The Bitter End

A Saints & Strangers Cozy Mystery

Book Three

Keeley Bates

Cover Design by Cover Kicks

Chapter One

Kit Wilder approached her ancestral home with caution. Although she preferred to keep the number of visits to Greyabbey to a minimum, her mother had sent word that an important piece of mail had arrived for her. Why Huntley, her mother's personal assistant, couldn't simply drop it off at Kit's house, she had no idea. Kit suspected it was another ploy to lure her back to Greyabbey for quality time.

The sound of hammering echoed through the trees and she spotted workers at the far end of the property line. She could only guess what her mother was up to. Probably erecting a wall to keep out the middle class.

Kit opened the front door without knocking and stepped into the impressive foyer.

"Hello," she called. "I've come for my important piece of mail. Be warned. If it's a Pottery Barn catalog, I'm going to strangle the nearest person holding a cocktail."

Huntley James emerged from a nearby reception room, his tall, effortlessly fashionable frame filling the doorway. "Good to see you, Sassafras," he said, waltzing over to kiss her cheek.

"Where are the dogs?" she asked, with a suspicious glance around the room. Hermès and Valentino, her mother's two Giant Schnauzers, were usually on hand to greet her and knock her on her backside.

"They're locked up right now," he told her. "Until the workmen leave."

"I noticed them. What's going on?"

"New fence around the perimeter," Huntley explained. "It needs to be at least five feet high."

Kit sighed. "Because four foot fences are so passé."

"Because a four foot fence won't contain Dexter, my wallaby," a voice shot back. Heloise Winthrop Wilder swept into the room, a Bloody Mary in one hand and a squirrel monkey perched on the other. "Dr. Nina says his leg is healing nicely and, once it does, look out."

"I'm sorry." Kit shook her head, thinking she'd misheard. "Did you say your wallaby?"

"Surely you've heard of a wallaby," Heloise said. "Yay high, jumps like a kangaroo."

Kit pursed her lips. "I know what a wallaby is."

"Then why act like you don't? Really, Katherine. Playing the dumb blonde? Is that what life in Hollywood does to you?"

"I'm a brunette," Kit replied hotly.

Heloise took a sip of her Bloody Mary. "And don't you forget it."

Kit watched in fascinated horror as the monkey grabbed the celery stick from her drink, took a bite and dumped the celery back into the glass.

"Dickens," Heloise scolded, yanking the glass out of reach. "You'd think he was raised in a barn."

"Or a rainforest," Kit added wryly.

The squirrel monkey protested loudly and jumped to the floor. Kit tried to hide her disgust when her mother took another sip of the Bloody Mary.

"Mother…"

Heloise gave her a withering look. "A little monkey urine is good for the complexion." She held out the glass. "What am I thinking? You need this more than I do. Here."

Kit vehemently shook her head. "He bit the celery. He didn't pee on it."

Heloise waved a dismissive hand. "Dickens likes to mark his path. He basically has urine all over his body."

Huntley snapped his fingers. "That reminds me. I need to wash the sheets." He retreated from the room with a slight bow.

"You said there's mail here for me?" Kit wanted to take the mail and run before she was peed on by a spider monkey or walloped by a wallaby.

"This way," her mother beckoned.

Kit followed her mother down the hall to the study.

"Have you finished for the holidays yet?" Heloise asked as she rifled through a stack of papers.

"Exams are this week and next, then we're done until the middle of January," Kit replied.

Heloise extracted a square, white envelope from the pile and handed it to Kit. "Here you are."

Kit studied the front. "An invitation?" she queried.

"A wedding invitation for Thomas Bitterbridge," her mother said.

"Here, lend me one of your claws." Kit handed her mother the envelope to open. Heloise slid a perfectly manicured nail across the back and opened the envelope.

"I always liked Tom," Kit remarked as she reviewed the elegant invitation. Close in age, Kit knew Tom pretty well from various social functions over the years. She knew he was engaged to Clara Pennypacker. Everyone in Westdale knew it, in fact, because the Bitterbridges and Pennypackers were mortal enemies. The Bitterbridges were old money Pilgrims like the Winthrops and the Wilders. The Pennypackers, on the other hand, had the bank account but not the lineage. Their wealth had been earned rather than inherited, a definite negative in the Pilgrim Society handbook.

"Too bad you're not marrying Tom instead of that Pennypacker girl," Heloise fretted. "Poor Betty. I've never seen a woman so constipated with rage."

"Then you're not looking in the mirror often enough."

Heloise lifted an eyebrow. "Betty hand-delivered these. The darling woman was seething when she was here last week. I had Huntley bring out the vials in case of a medical emergency."

"Is that your equivalent of smelling salts?" Kit pictured her mother's collection of vials, an eclectic assortment of anti-venom, painkillers, arsenic and other contraband.

"It wasn't a case of the vapors, thankfully," Heloise said. "Betty is made of stern stock, as you know."

"Why did she bring my invitation here?" Kit asked. "She knows I haven't lived here for years." Five years, in fact. Kit had left Westdale for Los Angeles at the ripe age of eighteen to pursue an acting career. After a very public downfall, she was back in Westdale in the role of college student, thanks to her mother's string-pulling.

"Did you expect her to risk life and limb in the ghetto?" Heloise asked, aghast. "It's not her fault you chose to live downwind."

"Downtown," Kit corrected her. "And it's hardly the ghetto." Thornhill Road was a lovely tree-lined street dotted with older, established homes. Kit had taken a lot of pride in fixing up her house, rescuing it from neglect and disrepair. "There are plenty of respectable people on my street."

"Plenty is a bit of a stretch," Heloise remarked.

Kit glanced at the wedding date. "Mother, this is Saturday!" She shook her head in disbelief. "I can't believe Betty delivered this last week."

"Oh, she didn't deliver *that* last week. She was just here to vent."

Kit eyed her mother suspiciously. "When exactly did Betty bring this invitation?"

Heloise stared dreamily into space. "I think it was during the Wimbledon semi-finals."

"Wimbledon," Kit repeated, incredulous. "That was months ago."

"No, no. Last year's Wimbledon."

Kit cringed. She couldn't believe that no one had mentioned the wedding to her. Her friends Francie and Charlotte had to be invited; both of their families had strong ties to the Bitterbridges.

"Your life was in such a state, Katherine," Heloise explained. "I was hardly going to send you a wedding invitation and rub your nose in someone else's socially acceptable happiness."

Kit doubted that her feelings were the only motive. It wasn't like Heloise to empathize with other humans.

"But I've been here for months now," Kit said. "Why wait until now to give it to me?"

"I was simply giving you time to hone your dancing skills, darling," Heloise said airily. "We all know that you take after your Grandmother Josephine when it comes to rhythm."

Kit studied her mother's guilty expression. "Baloney. You wanted to see if I'd have a respectable date by then. Since I don't, you want me to go alone."

Heloise made a noise at the back of her throat. "Well, I was going to caution you against bringing that new friend of yours."

Detective Romeo Moretti was Kit's new boyfriend, much to her mother's dismay. She took another look at the envelope. *Miss Katherine Clementine Winthrop Wilder and Guest* was clearly written on the front in elegant calligraphy.

"It isn't that I don't want you to bring him," her mother lied. "It's just that this is an opportunity to see what other Pilgrim stock is out there. You can't do that with a werewolf on your arm."

"A werewolf?"

"Sold build, dark and hairy, sniffs out clues," her mother said. "What else would he be?"

Kit narrowed her eyes and snatched the invitation from her mother's fingertips. "Thank you for letting me know about the wedding. I'll RSVP myself."

She stalked off toward the doorway.

"Watch out for Dexter on your way out," her mother called. "He likes to kick."

"The idiot has written a book." Kit stared at the television screen, her delicate jaw unhinged. The idiot in question was her former boyfriend and co-star, Charlie Owen.

"A fiction book?" Thora asked. Thora Breckenridge was Kit's octogenarian neighbor and fellow night owl. She'd started dropping by Kit's place when the evening talk shows kicked off, knowing that the actress-turned-college student would likely be awake and studying for exams.

"Everything out of the man's mouth is fiction," Kit griped. "I can only assume the same goes for his fingertips."

"I warned you not to watch," Jordan Newberg said, his angular face filling the screen of Kit's iPhone.

She jerked her head toward her best friend, who still served as the wardrobe designer for Kit's former television show, *Fool's Gold.* Through the magic of FaceTime, the friends were able to stay in daily contact.

"How can I not watch?" Kit asked. "The man is like a train wreck mixed with a car wreck and a helicopter crash on top."

"That sounds like good television," Thora mused.

"Now fans were devastated when Ellie Gold was killed off last year," the chubby-cheeked nighttime host said to Charlie and Kit's stomach clenched. Ever since Kit's character had been killed off, Charlie's popularity had soared. It seemed that the viewers liked him more when he suffered. They rooted for his character to overcome the untimely death of his beloved protégé and romantic partner. There had even been a poll for fans to choose which woman would make the best love interest for Jason now that Ellie Gold was gone. The busty medical examiner won, hands down.

"Yes," Charlie replied, "but you know, the writers have done an amazing job of keeping the show fresh. The viewers seem to have come around and embraced Jason's emotional journey this season."

"Oh sure," Kit complained to the television. "Kiss the writers' butts on network television. I know what you say about them behind their backs."

"You became quite close to Kit Wilder during her time on the show," the host remarked. "Have you been in touch with her since her shocking departure?"

Charlie had the decency to look contrite. "We're both busy people."

The host smiled, his jowls expanding even further. "So that's a no?"

"Well, she took the whole thing pretty hard so I figure it's best to give her space." He patted the front of the book. "But you can read all about our relationship in *Fool's Journey*, available in bookstores now."

"What?" Kit leapt from the sofa in outrage. "He wrote about me in that thing? Is he out of his mind?"

"Probably," Jordan said. "His dressing room is full of miniature bottles of alcohol. The kind you get on airplanes. I think he has a drinking problem. Or a hoarding problem. I'm not sure."

"Oh, he has a problem all right." Kit was fuming. How dare he write about their relationship! And then go on national television and talk about her. Why hadn't Beatrice, her bulldog of an agent, warned her that this was coming? Why hadn't…

"Jordan," she scolded, narrowing her eyes at the tiny screen. "You see the man almost every day. Didn't you know what he was up to?"

Jordan sank down so that Kit could only see the top of his spiky hair. "I didn't know. He kept it all very hush-hush."

Kit listened to the host lob a few more softball questions before clicking off the television.

"Should we start a Twitter feud?" Jordan asked, clearly hoping that the answer would be yes. "I have a few hashtags in mind already."

Kit shook her head. "I can't be bothered, not with exams this week. I hope his book tanks. I hope his whole career tanks." She threw a pillow at the television.

"He sure looked good in those tight jeans," Thora said. "Did he wear those jeans when he was with you?"

Kit didn't want to share the fact that Charlie preferred to prance around naked. If there was an opportunity to be without clothes, Charlie took to it like Heloise to a bottle of gin.

"Don't worry, Kit," Jordan said. "No one's going to buy his book. Everyone knows he must've used a ghostwriter because the man can't string two coherent sentences together."

Kit knew that Jordan was exaggerating for her sake. Charlie Owen was a charming, incredibly attractive man. A charming, incredibly attractive man who'd broken her heart.

She sighed in anguish. She'd already suffered through his betrayal in real life; she didn't need to relive it in print with the whole of America watching.

The wedding was held at Atlantica, the Pennypacker family's mega-mansion in Westdale. A seven-piece orchestra played in the background as women and men mingled in their finery. The ceremony in the Versailles-style gardens had seemed endless, not to mention chilly, and Kit was relieved to have reached the indoor drinking and eating part of the event.

She recognized many of the faces and was startled to notice that some of those faces looked younger than the last time she'd seen them at her father's funeral — more than five years ago.

"Do stop staring, Katherine," her mother instructed. "It's unseemly."

Kit blinked. "I'm not staring. I'm using the power of sight. Difficult to avoid with two working eyes."

"You look like you've never seen a facelift before, which we all know is pure poppycock given where you've been."

She meant Los Angeles. Her mother always spoke of L.A. like it was the tenth circle of hell.

"Hooray. There's Romeo," Kit said, brightening. She took advantage of his arrival and left her mother's side before another sour word dripped from her Chanel red lips.

He looked incredibly handsome in a classic tuxedo. His dark, wavy hair was neatly combed and his rugged jaw was clean-shaven. One look at him and she forgot all about her mother, Charlie Owen's book and her exams. He was a panacea for everything that was challenging in her life right now.

As Kit moved toward him through the throng of guests, heads turned to admire her pale skin encased in gold. She was, as usual, a striking vision that commanded attention.

"I'm sorry I had to miss the ceremony," he said, bending to kiss her cheek.

"Duty called, I understand."

"I'm glad you do. My last girlfriend wasn't so agreeable."

Kit understood the reality of a demanding job. She'd worked long hours on the set of *Fool's Gold*. She'd eaten all her meals on set because it got to the point where she didn't have time to go food shopping. It was no small wonder that she'd struck up a relationship with her co-star. Charlie was one of the few men she was able to spend significant periods of time with due to his close proximity on set.

"Katherine, so good of you to come."

"Mrs. Bitterbridge, congratulations," Kit said, plastering on a smile for the mother of the groom. Tom was her only child. As such, he was their only hope of carrying on the Bitterbridge name. Like many families in Westdale, propagating the line was a must. Kit knew that Tom had tremendous pressure on his shoulders. It couldn't have been easy to break the news to his parents that he was in love with a Pennypacker. Betty Bitterbridge was the kind of woman you didn't want to disappoint or upset. If Betty came out of the restroom with toilet paper stuck to the bottom of her shoe, Kit would walk away wordlessly rather than draw the woman's attention to it. As far as Betty Bitterbridge was concerned, no good deed went unpunished.

"So glad you could come at the last minute," Betty said.

"I wouldn't want to miss such a momentous occasion," Kit told her.

"A momentous occasion, indeed." Betty's frigid smile told Kit exactly how she felt about the union. Not that it came as a shock. Everyone in Westdale knew how upset the families were to join together in such an unholy matrimony. Frankly, Kit was surprised that the couple made it to the wedding with their relationship still intact.

Betty eyed Romeo. "And who is your guest?"

Romeo thrust out a strong hand. "Romeo Moretti, ma'am."

Betty stared at the hand with utter disdain. "I don't believe I know any Morettis."

"You would if you came to South Philly," he answered pleasantly. "There's a Moretti on every block."

Betty's upper lip curled and she backed away slowly, as though Romeo was an animal that might bite.

"How nice. I shall see to the Musgroves," Betty said absently. "Cecilia looks a bit lost in this extravagant excuse for a house. In my day, houses were wooden and symmetrical. None of these giant pillars and marble floors."

She wandered off, muttering angrily to herself.

Kit glanced up at Romeo to see how he handled the rejection. He leaned down and brushed his lips against hers.

"What a peach. Reminds me of your mother," he said and Kit laughed.

A flashbulb went off, momentarily blinding them both.

"Great smile. That'll be a keeper," the photographer said, tucking a strand of curly hair behind her ear.

"I thought the wedding party was still being photographed outside," Kit remarked.

"They are," the woman replied. "My husband is taking those." She extended a hand. "I'm Marina Lowe. Jacob and I run a photography studio together."

"Nice to meet you." Kit jerked her head toward Betty, who was lingering by the head table. "I take it she doesn't want to be photographed with her new daughter-in-law?"

Marina chuckled. "She's behaving herself. Her formal shots are done." Marina patted the phone protruding from her pocket. "Jacob and I are in constant contact."

"A well-oiled team," Romeo said approvingly. "I like it."

"You're not taking any videos?" Kit asked, noticing the absence of a video camera.

Marina shook her head, her dark curls bouncing around her face. "Video was expressly forbidden."

Kit guessed that people like the Bitterbridges and Pennypackers didn't want their more embarrassing moments on film. Embarrassing moments had a tendency to happen at open bar weddings.

Kit spotted her college friends, Francie Musgrove and Charlotte Tilton, across the room. "Let's say hello before my mother hunts me down. I don't know where she is, but I can feel her watching me with intense disapproval." She shrugged at Marina. "It's a gift."

Romeo took her hand and they crossed the room to join Francie and Charlotte.

"How's the studying going?" Francie asked.

"I'm thankful for a night out," Kit admitted. "My eyes are blurry from reading so much."

"Mine, too," Charlotte concurred. "I'm bumping into things more than usual." Charlotte had a condition called dyspraxia that made her prone to misjudging her surroundings. If there was a doorjamb or a table leg, Charlotte's elbow or toe was sure to catch it.

"The families seem to be fairly relaxed," Francie remarked. "My mother was sure there would be a major spectacle. I think I heard her praying for a dramatic objection during the ceremony."

"Well, the reception has only just started," Kit said. "There's still time."

"Ooh, food," Charlotte said, clapping her hands together. "Thank goodness. I'm starving."

Kit watched the servers set down small plates of hors-d'oeuvre next to flutes of champagne. Unsurprisingly, she saw her mother reach for a glass of champagne that was clearly meant to be used for the toast.

"Are you serious?" Kit muttered. "Girls, Romeo and I will be back. It seems an intervention is required."

"I'll leave the intervening to you," Romeo whispered. He knew better than to get between Heloise and alcohol.

After a brief dressing down of her mother, the music changed tempo and the bride and groom made their grand entrance. Kit thought that Clara was stunning in her second gown of the day, a strapless number with elaborate beading and feathers. She could see the pursed lips of the older women, silently condemning Clara's modern style. Tom, on the other hand, had never looked happier. The couple launched straight into their first dance and the crowd fell silent to watch them.

The speeches were as long and dull as Kit had anticipated. Mitch Pennypacker, the bride's father, was his usual pompous self, stopping just short of telling everyone exactly how much the day had cost him. Kit caught the look of disgust on her mother's face as he spoke. The Bitterbridges weren't alone in their dislike of the Pennypackers.

Once Mitch sat down, Betty pushed back her neighboring chair and stood. "I know it isn't customary for the mother of the groom to give a speech, but I would like to say a few words."

Tom nodded and Kit noticed a flash of surprise in his eyes.

"First, thank you to Pauline and Mitchell for hosting this wonderful event." She smiled politely at Mitch, who sat on her left, and then directed a curt nod at Pauline at the far end of the table. "For any mother, your child's wedding is inevitably a bittersweet day. You are losing your child to another family, in effect. Losing your son to another woman because the boy has finally become a man." She looked past Clara, who sat to her right, and gave Tom her full attention. "But know this, my son, I am not losing you today. Just because you are a man now doesn't mean I won't be here to support you, in good times and in bad. I will always be here, should you need me. I will always be your mother, no matter who else you meet in your life's journey. A mother who is immensely proud of her son."

It wasn't lost on Kit that there was no direct mention of the bride in Betty's speech. Kit could see the disappointment etched in Clara's pretty features. Still, it was a positive speech overall, especially considering the source. Their families had been feuding for decades, ever since Mitch bought the empty parcel of land between their estates to use as an airstrip for his private plane. Clara and Tom couldn't expect a miracle.

Tom cleared his throat and stood. "Thank you, Mother. To our family and friends, we thank you so much for respecting our love and agreeing to share our special day." He raised his champagne flute. "To our families and to many happy years together."

Kit raised her glass. Her gaze traveled around the room, drinking in the happy scene. She gave the young couple credit — Tom and Clara seemed to have accomplished the impossible.

A scream punctured the air and Kit swiveled toward the sound. A woman was slumped across the head table, gasping and jerking. Kit recognized the silver hair of Betty Bitterbridge. Clara had recoiled in horror but Mitch was beside her, calling her name in a panic.

"Somebody call 911," Tom yelled.

Romeo vaulted into action, scrambling around tables and chairs to reach the groom's mother before any of the other guests. Tip Bitterbridge remained at the opposite end of the table from his wife, stunned into paralysis.

Kit made it to the table in time to see Betty's last breath leave her parted lips. Her lithe body went slack.

"Romeo?" Kit placed a hand on his broad shoulder. Wordlessly, he shook his head.

"Mother!" Tom's voice was a pained shriek as he pushed past Clara to his mother's side, his face ashen. Flutes of champagne rolled off the table and dropped to the floor. The remaining liquid pooled on the expensive Shiraz carpet. Romeo took an unused, white linen napkin from the table and wrapped it around Betty's empty flute. Then he faced the wedding guests.

"I'll need everyone to sit down and remain calm," he announced. His deep voice rumbled through the room and bodies began to drop obediently into their chairs. "I don't want anyone to leave until emergency services arrive." He glanced at the empty flute in his hand. "And not to alarm anyone, but don't drink the champagne, just in case."

Kit heard the collective thump of glasses being set down on the tables. She stared at the side of Betty's face, her skin stretched in agony.

"Tom, I'm so sorry," Kit said. "We'll get to the bottom of this, I promise you."

Kit noticed Clara avert her gaze from her mother-in-law's body.

"You'll get to the bottom of nothing," Romeo said, his tone harsh and unyielding. "Kit, you should go back to the table and sit down like everyone else. Let me handle this."

"I'll do no such thing," she argued. "Mrs. Bitterbridge has dropped dead in front of one hundred and fifty people. We need to figure out what happened."

Romeo drew up to his full height, towering over Kit. "First of all, don't jump to conclusions."

"Says the man who palmed the champagne flute."

"We don't know that this is a murder," Romeo said. "She could've been ill. She could have had an allergic reaction to something in the food or drink."

Kit looked at Tip and Tom. "Did she have any known allergies?"

They shook their heads.

"Poor people," Clara said, without a trace of humor. "She was allergic to poor people, liberals and polyester."

"That's true," Tom agreed. "They all made her break out in hives."

"Well, this is clearly not a case of hives," Kit remarked, glancing down at the dead woman's body.

Romeo gripped Kit's arm. "Kit, I appreciate your interest, but you are not a detective. Please stop trying to act like one. Go back to your seat and let me do my job."

Kit stared into his dark eyes. She couldn't believe this was the same man she'd gotten to know these past few months. He was treating her the way her mother treated her, as incompetent and useless. She yanked her arm away and stepped back toward her table.

"Good luck," she called over her shoulder. As she snaked her way around the tables, she raised her chin a fraction. No need for people to see her upset. Not that anyone was watching her. All eyes were still fixed on the limp body of Betty Bitterbridge.

Kit slid into the seat beside her mother.

"I guess it's handy that you brought the wolf along after all," Heloise said.

"I can't believe this is happening," Charlotte said from across the table.

The doors burst open and emergency medical technicians flooded the room. Romeo whistled for them and Kit watched with a knot in her stomach as they confirmed what the wedding guests already knew. Betty Bitterbridge was officially dead.

Chapter Two

Kit lounged in the music room at Greyabbey after another marathon study session, a gin and tonic in one hand and a chocolate chip cookie in the other. Between Charlie's book, the wedding fiasco, exam pressure and Romeo's rebuke, Kit was feeling unusually delicate.

"That was the oddest wedding I've ever been to," Charlotte said. She sat on the floor with a psychology book in her lap, perfectly happy to be sandwiched between Hermès and Valentino.

"Poor Clara," Francie added. "I can't imagine what she must be feeling. Her wedding day was ruined."

"Leave it to a mother-in-law to ruin a bride's big day," Huntley chimed in from his position at the piano.

"The woman died," Kit pointed out. "She didn't order ugly flowers."

"Do you really think it was murder?" Charlotte asked, stroking Valentino's thick fur. She didn't like to think that Betty Bitterbridge was murdered in front of them. Her family and friends. It was brutal.

"Oh, it's most definitely murder," Huntley said matter-of-factly. "She was universally disliked by everyone, except for your mother, of course." He played a few notes of *Jingle Bells*.

"That might be a little too up-tempo, under the circumstances," Kit said, biting into the homemade cookie. God bless Diane and her secret recipes.

Huntley switched to the theme song from *Schindler's List*.

"That's more like it." Kit glanced at her iPhone on the table beside her. She hadn't heard from Romeo since he'd dismissed her at the wedding. She hoped he would call and apologize. Or at least confirm whether Betty's death was, in fact, murder.

"The current theory is poison," Heloise said, sweeping into the room with Miss Moneypenny in her arms. The white cat squirmed for its release but Heloise took no notice, only holding the cat closer to her chest.

Huntley stopped playing. "Why poison?" he asked. "Why not natural causes?"

"I'd rather not say," Heloise said, with a cursory glance at Francie and Charlotte, each with a cookie in hand.

"I'd rather you did," Kit insisted.

Huntley cleared his throat. "I think what your mother is trying to say is that there were bodily fluids in places where they shouldn't have been." Leave it to her mother's longtime personal assistant to decipher that code.

Kit swallowed a mouthful of gin and tonic. "Who told you that?" she asked her mother.

Heloise took a seat on the chaise lounge and Miss Moneypenny relaxed, curling up on her lap. "Richard, of course." As in Chief Rich Riley. She flicked a jeweled finger in Kit's direction. "You're not the only one with connections in the blue collar world, my dear."

"I'm surprised to hear you admit that out loud," Kit replied. "Won't you break out in a rash?" If only. "Did he say what kind of poison?"

"Not yet," Heloise replied. "They need to wait for the autopsy and then the toxicology report from the lab. Of course, with the holidays, nobody wants to work for a living."

"Heaven forfend!" Kit exclaimed. As if her mother had ever worked a day in her life.

"I almost told him to send me the evidence to speed things along," Heloise continued. "Dr. Nina is wonderful at identifying toxins."

"The vet?" Kit queried.

Heloise nodded enthusiastically. "She's saved many of the animals here when they've accidentally ingested something they shouldn't have."

Kit wasn't sure if she meant chocolate or one of her mother's hazardous materials. She didn't want to ask.

"What a way to kick off the holidays," Francie said.

"What a way to kick off their new life together," Charlotte said, thinking of Tom and Clara.

Kit couldn't help but feel sorry for herself. She glanced at her phone again, willing Romeo's name to appear on the screen. She prayed that Betty's last breath didn't signify the end of her relationship with the detective.

Kit stood at the top of a ladder in front of her house, attempting to hang Christmas lights for the first time in her life. She'd originally intended to ask Romeo for help, but that no longer seemed like a viable option. Besides, if ancient Thora Breckenridge somehow managed to decorate, then able-bodied Kit had no excuse.

As she lifted the lights higher, the cord got tangled in the bushes below. She yanked it but to no avail.

"Seriously?" she breathed. "This should be a cake walk." She'd filmed an episode of *Fool's Gold* where she had to scale the side of a building with a rope over her shoulder and succeeded in doing it in one take without a stunt double. It had been toward the end of season one and had marked the beginning of Charlie's personal interest in her. He'd stood below her during the scene and later confessed that it was the unobstructed view of her backside that convinced him to woo her. At the time, it had seemed charming.

"Looks like you could use a little help."

Kit craned her neck to where Phyllis Chilton sat in her mobility scooter in a robe and slippers. "Phyllis, it's like four o'clock. Why are you already dressed for bed?"

Phyllis moved her scooter up the driveway so that she could untangle the lights from the bushes. "I come over here in the bitter cold to help a neighbor in need and you take the time to criticize my outfit?"

"How do you expect to help me on a ladder when you refuse to acknowledge that you have full use of your legs?"

"Sometimes I wish you didn't have full use of your tongue," Phyllis replied.

Kit softened and resumed her hanging of the lights. "I'm sorry. I'm just grouchy. There's a lot going on."

"The Italian Stallion?"

She nodded. "We had a disagreement."

At that moment, a familiar black car turned the corner and pulled behind Kit's car in the driveway.

"It's like I summoned him," Phyllis said, staring at the car in awe.

"Ladies," Romeo said, emerging from the car. "Can I offer some assistance?"

"Absolutely not," Kit replied, stubbornly turning back toward the exterior of the house.

Romeo raised his thick eyebrows at Phyllis, who only shrugged.

"I'll be in my house if you need me, binge-watching *Outlander*." Phyllis hugged herself. "I wish somebody would send me back to eighteenth century Scotland. I love a man in a kilt." She eyed Romeo. "You've got the legs for it."

"Um, thank you?" He waited until Phyllis rolled back across the street before trying to address Kit. He could tell it was going to be a challenge.

"What brings you here?" Kit asked.

"And here I thought it was just the weather that was frosty."

Kit refused to look at him. He'd humiliated her in front of friends and family and made her feel worthless. She couldn't let it go.

"I'm sorry that I gave you a hard time," he said, gripping the base of the ladder.

Kit continued stringing the lights across the edge of the roof.

"Kit, I know you've helped me in the past and I appreciate it, but the reality is that you're not a cop. Not a detective. You're Kit Wilder, not Ellie Gold. You should focus on your schoolwork. Be who you really are."

She twisted toward him. "In other words, get back in my box."

"Yes," he said, then shook his head in confusion. "No."

Kit gritted her teeth and faced the house again. "Have I or have I not helped you solve two murders?"

"You have, but…"

"But nothing," Kit interrupted. "Please don't act like I'm some bimbo who stumbled into the truth. Twice."

"You're not a bimbo," Romeo said firmly.

"Good, then tell me what the medical examiner said."

He sighed. "The preliminary autopsy report says heart attack."

"What about the poison theory?" she asked. "The bodily fluids?"

"Dare I ask where you heard that?" He pressed his lips together. "Forget it. I can make an educated guess." Kit heard the note of resignation in his voice. "The heart attack could have been brought on by the poison. There won't be a final determination until the toxicology report comes in."

"Any suspects?"

Romeo hesitated. "We've arrested Clara."

Kit spun around so quickly that she nearly fell off the ladder. "You what?"

Romeo thrust his hands in his pockets. "She had means, motive and opportunity."

"She was the bride," Kit yelled, climbing down to confront him. "Of course she had unfettered access to all things wedding related. So did Tom. So did Tip. So did Clara's parents and her brother."

Romeo struggled to maintain his composure. "We have a witness who claims that Clara and Betty had several heated arguments leading up to the wedding and that Clara was adamant about keeping the booze flowing in Betty's direction. We've also sent Betty's champagne flute to be tested for any poisonous residue."

"You think Clara poisoned Betty's champagne?"

He shrugged. "It's one theory. With a domineering mother-in-law out of the way, Clara is now the matriarch of that very influential family. She also knows in great detail all of the efforts made by Betty Bitterbridge to stop the wedding before it happened."

"Betty didn't exactly hide her antipathy," Kit said, climbing down the ladder.

"Well, it seems Clara decided not to hide hers either."

Kit pressed her fingers to her temples. There was no way that sweet Clara Pennypacker murdered her mother-in-law. Certainly not at her own wedding.

She looked Romeo in the eye. "Romeo, you have to trust me. There is no way that Clara is the murderer."

Romeo gave an exasperated sigh and lifted his gaze to the darkening sky. "Kit, I really want to make things work with you, but not if you can't let things go. You want me to trust you. Why don't you trust me to do *my* job?"

"Clara is innocent," Kit insisted. "And I can prove it."

Romeo groaned and paced the lawn in front of her. "I don't want you to prove anything, Kit. I wasn't planning to tell you anything about the case, but then I figured you'd just wheedle it out of Harley or Jamison anyway." His eyes pleaded with her. "I'm asking you one last time to stay out of it."

Kit closed her eyes, already kicking herself. "I can't. Not when you have the wrong person."

Romeo cursed under his breath. He'd prayed that she'd make the sensible choice. The one he wanted her to make. He didn't want the relationship to fall apart before it really got started. "I knew you wouldn't agree. That Owen guy calls you stubborn and righteous. Boy was he on to something."

Kit gaped at him. "Charlie Owen?"

Romeo wished he could snatch back the words. He had no intention of telling Kit that he'd bought a copy.

Her eyes narrowed. "You read his book."

His shoulders slackened. "Technically, I'm still reading it. Haven't finished yet."

"He calls me stubborn and righteous?" Her voice grew small.

Romeo reached for her, but she backed away. "Kit…"

A shadow passed across her face and she turned back toward the house. "Thanks for stopping by, but I have an exam to study for. Have a good evening, Romeo."

He followed her up the front steps but she was too quick. The door slammed in his face and he cringed when he heard the lock click into place.

"Kit," he said, knocking softly. "Open up."

She refused to open the door unless she heard an apology. Eventually, she heard the motor start and listened as the car eased out of the driveway. Her studies would have to wait. Right now, it seemed that Kit had a different book to read.

Kit sat in the back booth of Provincetown Pancakes with Francie and Charlotte for their evening study session. Their course review, however, inevitably turned to talk of Betty Bitterbridge.

"I don't how the police could suspect Clara," Charlotte said. "She wouldn't hurt a fly."

"She did instruct the staff to keep Betty's glass full at all times," Francie said. "That much was confirmed. Even my mother heard her."

"So she wanted Betty drunk," Kit said. "Big deal. Everyone in Westdale knows that Betty likes her medicine. I'm sure Clara knew it, too, and wanted to use it to sideline her."

"Can you blame her?" Charlotte added. "I'd be quaking in my boots if Betty Bitterbridge was about to become my mother-in-law."

"Especially after all of Betty's efforts to break them up," Francie added.

"My mother mentioned once that Betty asked to borrow a few pets." Kit shoved a forkful of cranberry pancakes into her mouth and sighed blissfully. It was holiday heaven. "She seemed to think that a well-placed snake and a few monkeys might scare Clara off."

Charlotte nodded vigorously. "That would be enough to get rid of me."

"Did she actually borrow them?" Francie asked.

Kit shook her head. "Mother didn't trust Betty to take proper care of them. She was afraid that Josephine would end up in a sewer."

"Josephine is the snake?" Francie queried.

"Isn't that your grandmother's name, too?" Charlotte asked.

Kit smiled. "And you think Clara is the only one with mother-in-law problems?"

"Well, no matter what the police think, there is no way that Clara killed Betty. I mean, you both saw the gown she wore. She would have needed to strap a bottle of poison to her garter belt," Francie said.

Kit nodded. "I had the same thought. And that she somehow lifted that enormous skirt of hers at the head table and removed the bottle or vial or whatever she kept it in, and poured the poison into Betty's glass."

"Not to mention, Clara and Tom were the last people to enter the reception," Francie pointed out. "There's no way she could have done it. Everyone was already seated at the table."

"If the bride is lifting up her dress, people are going to notice." Charlotte sipped her tea.

"They were sitting next to each other, though," Francie said. "I suppose Clara could've had the poison ready in her hand and secretly dumped it in."

"No," Kit objected. "Clara and Tom had their first dance before they sat down. If she'd had something clutched in her hand, he would've noticed."

"What about her father?" Francie asked. "Mitch sat on the other side of Betty. His arm is certainly long enough to reach her glass. God knows it was long enough to try to feel me up from several seats away at the cancer fundraiser last month." She shuddered and took a bite of her waffle.

"Did the police find the empty container of poison that Clara supposedly had?" Francie asked.

Kit shook her head. "I spoke to Harley and managed to extract that much out of him."

"How did you do that?" Charlotte asked. "I thought he'd be afraid of Romeo."

"He is, but I offered him an autographed copy of Charlie's book if he told me." She shrugged. "He's a huge fan."

"How are you dealing with that?" Francie asked. "I've been afraid to bring it up."

"Romeo or the book?"

"Both," Francie replied.

"I'm still deciding," Kit replied. "And I won't know what to do until I decide how I feel."

"If you want help, just say the word," Francie said, straightening in her seat.

"Thanks," Kit replied, "but I think this is something I need to handle on my own."

Kit was alerted to the arrival of the new neighbors when the sound of a moving truck roused her from a mid-day nap. She'd taken her psychology exam at nine that morning and had come home to power nap before her next exam at two. She couldn't wait for the semester to be over. After all her hours of studying, she was ready for a break.

She opened the bedroom window and poked her head out for a better view. *Smooth Moves* was emblazoned on the side of the truck. Moving men were carrying furniture into the house, but there was no sign of the new owners.

Kit was still dressed from this morning, so she simply ran a brush through her hair and secured it with a ponytail. At the very least, she thought she should look presentable for their first meeting. She sure hoped they were better neighbors than the last woman who lived there. Peregrine Monroe was the epitome of prim and proper. Kit was glad when she moved to Sedona not long after Kit moved in.

She hopped down the stairs and grabbed a fleece before venturing out into the cold. She could see her breath as she made her way down the front steps and across the lawn.

Two movers went by, carrying a large sofa. One of them stopped dead when he saw Kit standing on the other side of the bushes and nearly got steamrolled by the sofa.

"Marco, what are you doing, man?" the other guy hissed.

Marco was still staring at Kit. "Holy Doritos. It's Ellie Gold, right?"

Kit gave a rueful smile. "I got your bling right here."

Marco dropped his end of the sofa and clapped his hands. "I can't believe it. Gomez, do you know who this is?"

Gomez set down the other end of the sofa and eyed Kit. "I guess her name's Ellie Gold since that's what you called her."

"It's Kit, actually," she said. "I played a character on TV called Ellie Gold."

"*Fool's Gold*, amigo," Marco said. "Man, I love that show. I was so pissed when you died. I threw a cup at the screen and stained the rug. Maria was not happy with me."

"You died?" Gomez queried.

Kit shrugged. "Personality conflict."

"And now you live here?" Marco asked. He glanced over her shoulder to assess the house she stepped out of. "I guess you're doing okay."

Kit smiled. "I'm doing better than okay." Even though the house wasn't anywhere near as nice as Greyabbey or her place in L.A., she knew she was fortunate to live here.

"This is so cool," Marco said. He pulled a phone from his jeans pocket. "Would you mind taking a picture with me? My friends will go loco."

Kit was glad she'd made an effort to freshen up before coming outside. She skirted the bushes and came to stand beside Marco who handed the phone to Gomez.

"You take it, broja."

Marco slung his arm over Kit's shoulders and grinned at the camera phone. Her smile was less exuberant due to lack of sleep, but it was there.

"Making friends with the rabble," Thora said, her petite frame cutting across the front lawn. "What would your mother say?" She stopped to admire the movers as they lifted the sofa once again. Her pale blue eyes traveled down one's bicep and up the other's thigh. It didn't matter that they were in multiple layers of clothing.

Kit shuddered. "Stop it, Thora. I can feel you undressing them. It's gross."

"Nothing gross about it," Thora replied. "Having seen it up here, I can assure you." She tapped her temple.

A woman with dark, curly hair appeared on the front step, checking on the movers' progress. She broke into a broad smile when she spotted Kit and Thora.

"I can see the reason for the slowdown," she called as she maneuvered past the movers and approached them. "Hi, I'm Sofia Alvarez." She cocked her head at Kit. "You must be the actress."

"Kit Wilder," she said.

"Myra Beacon told us that we were moving next door to Westdale royalty," Sofia said.

"That Myra will say anything to sell a house," Thora sniffed. "I'm surprised she didn't tell you the toilet was gold-plated."

"This is my neighbor," Kit said apologetically. "Thora Breckenridge. Her house is there." She pointed to the house on the other side of hers.

"Nice to meet you, Thora." She paused to watch the movers lift a large piece of furniture. Once they were safely through the doorway, she turned back to the women. "Sorry, I needed to keep an eye on that one. It's an antique."

"Do you live alone?" Kit asked.

"Only in my dreams," Sofia replied with a laugh. "Oh God. That sounded awful. No, I have two children and my husband is a lawyer. He's working now, unfortunately. That's why I'm here overseeing the move."

"How old are your kids?" Kit asked. She thought it would be a nice change for Thornhill Road to have a couple of kids on the block.

"My son is four and my daughter is eight. They're with my parents right now. We're staying with them until after the holidays. Then I need to be here for work."

"In Westdale?" Thora inquired.

Sofia nodded. "I'm teaching at Westdale College."

Kit's eyes lit up. "That's where I go to school."

Sofia wrapped her cardigan more tightly around her waist to stave off the chill. "That's great. What's your major?"

"Psychology," Kit answered. "I'm about to finish my first semester."

"I teach criminal justice."

Kit and Thora exchanged meaningful glances. "God knows we could use a bit of expertise around here," Thora said.

Sofia's brow creased. "Really? I thought Westdale was ridiculously safe. That's one of the main reasons the job appealed to me." She shrugged. "That and my parents. We've been living in Pittsburgh and my parents were desperate to have us closer to them."

"I know the feeling," Kit said, thinking of Heloise. Her mother had revoked her trust fund when Kit decided to move to Los Angeles in an effort to force her to stay in Westdale. Heloise's vengeance had backfired, however. It only made Kit determined to succeed without the family's money. "Well, Westdale is relatively safe."

"But when it isn't, you get the benefit of meeting the hottest detective this side of the Mississippi." Thora wiggled her eyebrows.

Kit elbowed her gently in the ribs. "Can we not talk about Romeo, please?"

"You should take her class," Thora urged, gesturing to Sofia. "It could be useful."

Sofia fixed her gaze on Kit. "Useful?"

Kit's cheeks turned pink. "I like to help out when there's a murder investigation. I guess I'm having a hard time leaving my character behind."

"Your character was a murderer?" Sofia asked, surprised.

"No, a detective. *Fool's Gold*," she said.

Sofia smiled politely. "I don't watch police procedurals. They get too many things wrong and it drives me crazy."

"It wasn't quite a police procedural," Kit said. She heard the defensive tone in her voice, but she couldn't help it. "The show was more about the characters."

"I like medical dramas," Sofia told them. "Were you in any of those?"

Kit shook her head.

"I star in one of those at least once a week," Thora quipped. "You're welcome to accompany me to an appointment. In fact, I have a gynecology visit tomorrow."

"Mrs. Alvarez," Marco called from the front step. "We have a question about where you want that armoire. We don't think it's going to fit."

Sofia inhaled deeply. "Back to business. It was nice meeting you both. We'll need to have you over for coffee after the holidays. Once we're settled."

"Let us know if you need help with anything," Kit said.

"Let *her* know," Thora added. "I'm just a feeble old woman."

"Faker," Kit shot back. "You're the least feeble woman I know."

Sofia crossed the lawn and returned to her house to advise the movers. Once she was out of earshot, Kit glanced sidelong at Thora. "When's the last time you had kids living on this street?"

Thora tapped her chin with her index finger. "Twenty years?"

"This is going to be a nice change for the neighborhood." Heloise could say what she liked about the domino effect of Kit's purchase of a foreclosure. Kit loved the idea of a young family finally finding an affordable house in Westdale. It was about time, too.

"As long as they stay out of my garden," Thora grumbled.

"I'm sure you'll get your point across if you brandish your antique revolver." Kit shivered from the cold. "I'm going inside to rest up and clear my mind."

"Don't clear it too much," Thora warned. "You need to actually answer the exam questions."

Kit stuck out her tongue before retreating into the house. The truth was, she was having a hard time keeping her mind on her study guide. How could she focus on statistics when what she really wanted to do was figure out who killed Betty Bitterbridge?

Kit wasted no time after her final exam. Instead of celebrating the end of the semester with her fellow students, she drove straight to Oakheart, the Bitterbridge estate. If there was any way she could help reunite Tom and Clara, then she intended to find it.

She drove Betsy, her red Corvette Stingray, up the long, winding drive that led to Oakheart. She'd heard from Diane, the housekeeper at Greyabbey, that Tom was living in the family home again. Diane and Dora, the Bitterbridge housekeeper, were old friends and met for coffee once a week, presumably to complain about their respective employers.

The heavy wooden doors of Oakheart were like something from a medieval castle. Kit thought that a moat wouldn't have seemed entirely out of place at the Bitterbridge home.

"Good to see you again, Miss Wilder," Dora said with a hesitant smile. "I take it you're here to see young Tom."

"I am. Is he presentable?"

Dora's brow wrinkled. "As presentable as you're going to get, I'm afraid. Come with me."

Kit followed Dora down a wood-paneled hallway to a back staircase. "Up the stairs," Dora instructed. "First door on the right."

"Thank you." Kit took the stairs two at a time in an effort to squeeze in a bit of cardio. She'd been exercising less and less as the town transitioned into colder weather. She wasn't used to the winter seasons anymore. In Los Angeles, winter meant rain and a fashionable jacket. Winter in Westdale meant functional hats, scarves, gloves and boots. It had everything to do with staying warm and nothing to do with looking good.

She knocked on the bedroom door, but there was no answer. "Tom?"

Kit waited a moment before knocking again. A more urgent knock garnered no response. She began to worry about Tom's state of mind. His mother was dead and his new wife was the prime suspect. What if he'd decided to take matters into his own hands?

She pushed open the door, her heart thumping wildly in her chest. Her concern was unfounded. There was Tom, slumbering peacefully in his bed. Kit sighed with relief and leaned against the doorjamb.

The room was vaguely familiar. His walls were adorned with posters of *A Clockwork Orange* and *2001: A Space Odyssey*. In one slovenly corner, his cricket equipment laid in a pile on the floor. Not quite the man that his mother had described in her wedding speech. Not in his childhood bedroom, anyway.

Tom stirred.

"Hi, Tom," she said softly.

He rubbed his eyes and sat up, trying to rouse himself. "Yes? Dora?"

Kit stepped further into the room. "No, it's Kit. I wanted to speak with you about your mother and Clara."

Tom stretched and yawned, not bothered in the least by Kit's unexpected presence. "The police have come to their senses and decided to release her?"

Tom gave her a sleepy smile, but the smile quickly faded when he took notice of Kit's sober expression. He straightened his wiry frame and put on his glasses, ready to talk.

"We can go downstairs, if you'd be more comfortable there," Tom suggested.

"I'm fine here if you are. You might not remember, but I've been in here a few times before."

Tom broke into a smile. "How could I forget? I had such a crush on you when we were kids."

"We played Go Fish until the wee hours of the morning."

"So our parents could drink like fish," Tom added. "Your father liked scotch and soda and your mother prefers gin." His eyes met Kit's. "How long has it been?"

Kit knew exactly what he meant. "More than five years now." Her father, Douglas Wilder, had been dead for more than five years. A heart attack on the golf course.

"Does it ever get easier?"

Kit gave him a sympathetic smile. "No, but you learn to cope."

"Your father was different, though. He wasn't like the others." His chin trembled faintly. "He certainly wasn't like Mother."

"I've often wondered what my parents saw in each other," Kit admitted. "My dad was so salt-of-the-earth and my mother is...not of this earth. The only things they had in common were money and a Pilgrim heritage."

"They say opposites attract." His smile faded. "Clara and I aren't opposites, though. We have a lot in common."

Kit perched on the edge of his desk. "Your families are opposites, though. The Pennypackers represent everything that the Bitterbridges hate."

"True enough," Tom agreed. "When I first met Clara in college, I avoided her like the plague. I thought she'd be vulgar and want to talk about her plane and her yacht all the time."

"You came by that impression honestly," Kit said. She remembered plenty of Pennypacker events that included grand and ostentatious displays of wealth. Atlantica had a separate residence for staff that Kit found reminiscent of slave quarters in the pre-Civil War South. Her own father disliked Mitch Pennypacker, which was telling. At the Westdale Country Club, Mitch apparently spent a lot of time at the bar, boasting about his latest multimillion dollar toy. Doug Wilder didn't like to talk about money, not because he was too classy but because he felt guilty about having so much of it.

"It was a fashion show that changed my mind," Tom said. "She organized a charity event to raise money for orphans of war." He smiled at the memory. "I assumed, of course, that her real purpose in organizing it was to take center stage and walk away with an armful of new designer clothes."

"But she didn't?"

He shook his head. "She didn't even walk in the show. She stayed behind the scenes, running the whole event flawlessly." He glanced up at Kit and she noticed tears shining in his eyes. "At the cocktail party afterward, she had dark circles under her eyes and her hair was a mess, but she was so proud of the money she'd raised that she couldn't be bothered to fix herself up. I fell in love with her right then and there."

The more Tom spoke, the more Kit was convinced that Clara had nothing to do with Betty's murder. Clara didn't seem capable of that level of hatred or spite.

"She sounds lovely," Kit agreed.

"I know she's innocent, Kit." His jaw set. "I can't speak for anyone else in her family, but it definitely wasn't Clara."

"I believe you." She cocked her head. "Then who else? Mitch Pennypacker was seated next to your mother. Do you think it could have been him?"

"I wouldn't want to speculate. It's hard to have an unbiased opinion about a man my family has avoided like the plague for decades."

"Who also happens to be your new father-in-law."

Suddenly Kit heard footsteps thumping up the stairs and was shocked to see Clara Pennypacker appear in the doorway. Black mascara streaked across her cheeks and her clothes were wrinkled, but her smile was radiant.

"Tom!" she cried and launched herself into his arms.

"Clara," he replied in disbelief. He kissed her and held her close. "What happened? They released you?"

"They did," she said.

"What convinced them?" Tom asked.

"My father. And my brother, too."

"What do you mean?" Tom asked and lowered his voice. "How did they convince them?"

Kit knew what he was implying. Mitch Pennypacker was the type of man who wouldn't bat an eye over offering bribes. Generous bribes.

"They've confessed," she proclaimed.

Kit's mouth dropped open. "They confessed?"

She nodded. "They didn't actually do it, silly. My father said he acted alone and so did Steven. It was Daddy's lawyer's idea. He said Chief Riley couldn't untie a knot in his shoelace, let alone a knot like this one."

"I'll bet," Kit said. She noticed that Tom remained silent.

Clara kissed his cheek. "Isn't it wonderful, Tom? Now we can be together. Get your things so we can go home. I can't leave town until things are settled with Daddy and Steven, so our honeymoon is still on hold, but we'll get to Fiji soon enough." She felt Tom stiffen in her arms. "Tom, what is it?"

"Clara, I know you're innocent, but I can't say the same about your family. What if your father or your brother is using this as an opportunity to get away with murder?" He grimaced. "My mother's murder."

Clara withdrew from his embrace and stared at him. "Tom, my family would never betray me like that. What ever you may think of the Pennypackers, we're not coldblooded killers."

"I don't think poorly of the Pennypackers," Tom insisted.

"I think you do," Clara countered, rising to her feet. "I think your prejudice goes deeper than you realize, Thomas Alexander Bitterbridge. It's bad enough to not be a Saint in this town, but to not be a Stranger either." She drew a breath. "Your mother's prejudices have infected you more than you realize."

"Be that as it may," Tom said, "if your family members have confessed to my mother's murder, whether I believe it or not, I can't be with you, Clara. How can I be part of a family who's taken responsibility for killing my mother? Married to a woman who's content to let the real killer remain free by playing the system?"

Clara recoiled, visibly hurt. "I'm not protecting the real killer, Tom. I'm telling you — no Pennypacker did this. You need to look elsewhere."

"Kinda difficult for the police to look elsewhere when two different Pennypackers have confessed," he murmured. "They won't be looking for the real killer if they're too busy untangling Pennypacker lies."

Tears streamed down Clara's cheeks. "I thought they were doing the right thing. Daddy and Steven want to help me. Help us. I would think you'd appreciate that."

"They did it to protect you, Clara," Tom said. "Or possibly themselves. Don't be naive. It's not about me or my family. They should step back quietly if they want the real murderer brought to justice."

"You're my husband, Tom. I'm not just a Pennypacker anymore. I'm a Bitterbridge, too. And I'm willing to do anything to be with you."

A shadow passed over Tom's face. "And that's exactly what worries me the most."

Chapter Three

Kit knew that it would be a mistake to pester Romeo with questions about the Pennypackers' confessions, so she decided to take matters into her own hands. In season four of *Fool's Gold*, Ellie and her team were up against a notorious Russian crime family. Nobody in the family would talk to the police because the consequences of talking were worse than the consequences of remaining silent. Although Kit didn't think the Pennypackers were going to be driving nails through anybody's feet and hands, they had closed ranks when one of their own was accused, just like the Ivankov family. Naturally, Ellie had managed to sniff out a weak link in the chain, an uncle dying of lung cancer who no longer wanted to damn his eternal soul. Kit decided to sniff out an Uncle Viktor.

She changed into her tennis whites and headed for the Westdale Country Club. From what she could gather, Mitch Pennypacker's ego was the weak link. If she knew Mitch, he'd be in his usual spot at the bar, boasting about his family's clever plan to outwit Lady Justice. Whether he realized it or not, he was also going to destroy his daughter's marriage in the process and Kit didn't want to see that happen. Tom and Clara were so in love; it would be horrible if Betty's death drove a permanent wedge between them.

Kit heard his voice before she even saw him, laughing loudly and slapping his knee. The bartender didn't look nearly as amused as Mitch did. Kit quickly pinched her cheeks for color and sauntered into the room. Mitch would talk; he always talked. It was getting him to reveal anything useful that would prove the real challenge.

"I'll have a sparkling water with lemon, please," she told the bartender.

"If it isn't Katherine Winthrop Wilder," Mitch Pennypacker declared. "I heard you were at the wedding of the decade. I apologize for not making the rounds, but I'm sure you understand."

"Good afternoon, Mr. Pennypacker," she said, sidling up to the bar. "No apology needed. It was a harrowing day. I'm somewhat surprised to see you here under the circumstances."

Mitch blew a raspberry. "Then you put too much faith in the Westdale criminal justice system."

"Clearly, they didn't arrest you."

He grinned in a way that made Kit want to slap him across the face. God, he was smug. "Not enough evidence. You see, a confession isn't enough. They need to find corroborating evidence, but they'd need to take their heads out of each other's asses long enough to find any."

"And now they're chasing two competing leads," Kit said.

He saluted her with his drink.

"Aren't you worried that the police might actually uncover enough evidence to arrest you or Steven and take it to trial?"

Mitch chuckled. "They're welcome to try."

Kit wondered whether the real killer would be so blasé. Possibly, if he knew he'd covered his tracks. Or if he was as wealthy and arrogant as Mitch Pennypacker.

"I heard if they can't find evidence, they'll file obstruction of justice charges against you and Steven," she lied.

His expression darkened. "Let them. How much will that set me back? A week in Monaco? Lord knows Chief Riley is in enough people's pockets around here. He'll learn that my pocket is bigger than the rest of them combined."

Kit bit back a groan. Her father had been right. Mitch really was insufferable.

"The police seem to be working round the clock on this, though." She guessed, anyway. If Romeo were speaking to her, she could confirm it as a fact.

"It's like Abbott and Costello," Mitch boomed. "The left hand doesn't know what the right hand is doing."

"And which hand am I?" a voice asked.

Kit whipped around to see Officers Lucas Harley and Brian Jamison behind them. Young and inexperienced, Kit had developed a fondness for both officers over the past few months.

"Hello gentlemen," she said. "What brings you to this fine establishment?"

"Same as you, I suspect," Harley whispered, brushing past her. "Mr. Pennypacker, we've been following up on some of the statements you made to Detective Moretti and we're hoping you can answer a few more questions."

"Not without my lawyer," he said, throwing back the rest of his drink.

"Your lawyer said you would cooperate with the investigation," Jamison reminded him, blowing a strand of red hair out of his eye. "That's all this is."

"Miss Wilder, would you mind giving us a minute with Mr. Pennypacker?" Harley asked.

"She very much minds," Mitch replied. He stood and took Kit by the elbow. "Katherine and I have a scheduled tennis match and we cannot be late. Club rules, you understand."

Kit gave the officers a helpless shrug as he dragged her away.

Mitch escorted Kit as far as the doorway that led to the changing rooms when she turned back. "Excuse me one minute. I seem to have left my handbag behind."

She bolted back to the bar where Harley and Jamison were speaking with the bartender about Mitch.

"Romeo is not going to like this," Jamison whispered.

"So don't tell him," she hissed.

"Mitch Pennypacker could easily be a coldblooded killer," Jamison added.

"Only one way to find out," Kit said and winked as she trotted back to Mitch.

"Do you really intend to play tennis?" Kit asked. "I wouldn't object. As it happens, my partner cancelled at the last minute." No need for Mitch to know that he was the only reason she was there.

Mitch eyed her tennis whites. "I'll admit, I haven't played a good game in ages. The men my age can't keep up with me." He loosened his shoulders and rolled his neck from side to side. "You look like you're in pretty good shape."

"I do okay." Kit flashed him an innocent smile. She didn't feel the need to tell him about her years of training with Hans, her trainer and stunt coordinator for *Fool's Gold.* She'd had years of tennis practice growing up in Westdale, but Hans had taught her how to win. At everything.

Sensing Mitch's own eagerness to win combined with his bravado, an idea began to form. "I'll tell you what," she said. "If I win, you tell me something about the day of the murder that you haven't already told the police." Assuming there was something. It was a gamble, but she decided to take it.

"And here I thought we'd play for cash given your lack of a trust fund," he said. Her mother's revocation of her trust fund was common knowledge in Westdale.

"I have enough money," she answered. "I'm more interested in having information that no one else knows." She gave him a flirtatious wink. "For the thrill of it."

"And what if I win?" She noticed his gaze moving down her bare legs and inwardly shuddered. Murderer or not, Mitch Pennypacker was repulsive in every way.

"I'll tell you something I know about the murder," she replied. "Something you could use to your advantage."

"And how would you have access to information that I don't?" he asked, his arms crossed.

"Let's not forget who my date was to your daughter's wedding," she pointed out.

"I heard he dumped you," Mitch said and Kit bristled.

"Well, let's not forget who my mother is," she said. "Her well-placed sources are legendary." It wasn't a lie. As the head of the centuries-old Pilgrim Society, Heloise could usually be found in the eye of every storm in Westdale and everyone knew it. Mitch was no exception.

He held out his hand. "Deal."

As Mitch headed to the changing room, Kit tried not to show her satisfaction. She didn't need to be on the tennis court to know that she'd already won.

Kit was on the hunt for a redhead. Her win over Mitch on the tennis court had yielded a single clue — a waitress who allegedly saw Mitch pour the still unnamed poison into Betty's champagne glass in the kitchen. Even if the waitress confirmed his story, though, Kit wasn't completely satisfied. She'd posed a litany of questions that Mitch had refused to answer. How was he sure that the correct glass would be delivered to Betty? Did he pay a server to set the poisoned glass at Betty's place at the head table? If so, did the server know what he or she was doing? What kind of poison was it and where did Mitch obtain it? As far as Mitch was concerned, he'd fulfilled his end of the bargain so Kit was back in action, following up on the one lead he provided.

Kit pulled into the small parking lot of Calliope Catering. It was a newer business in Westdale so Kit didn't know anyone affiliated with the company. She hoped she could get them to speak to her without Romeo by her side. Then again, she'd done well enough on her own so far. A small part of her hoped Romeo would be more impressed than angry.

As she stepped out of the car, she was immediately slapped in the face by the frigid air. She still hadn't fully adjusted to winter weather. It would probably be April by the time she'd accepted it.

Kit pushed open the door and inhaled the scent of freshly baked bread.

"Wow. That smells amazing," Kit said, smiling brightly at the girl behind the counter. If anything could cheer her up, it was delicious carbs.

"Holy cow. You're Kit Wilder," the young woman said, giddy with excitement. "People said you were at the Pennypacker wedding, but I didn't believe them."

"That's actually why I'm here," she said. "Would it be possible to speak to the members of staff who worked the event?"

"All of them?" the young woman queried.

"I'm looking specifically for a redhead."

The young woman's face lit up. "That's Bonnie. She's in the back. Hold on and I'll get her." She hustled to the back room and returned moments later with a freckled woman. There was no mistaking the red hair. It was like wearing a crown of fire.

"Hi, Bonnie. I'm Kit Wilder."

Bonnie couldn't stop grinning. "I know who you are. I loved you on *Fool's Gold.* I couldn't believe they killed you off like that. So rude."

Kit shrugged. "That's the business."

Bonnie continued on. "I read Charlie Owen's book, you know. I wanted to see if he was sorry for what he did to you, that two-timing jerk."

Kit's stomach tightened. She didn't want to talk about Charlie Owen, certainly not with a stranger in Calliope Catering.

"I'm not really here to discuss my career." She cleared her throat. "Or my personal life. I understand that you worked the Pennypacker wedding."

Bonnie nodded. "It was such a beautiful wedding." Her pale skin grew even paler, making her freckles pop. "Until that awful thing happened."

"Yes, that awful thing. Betty Bitterbridge's murder."

Bonnie visibly shuddered. "She wasn't a nice woman, but still…"

Bonnie would get no argument from Kit there. "Mitch Pennypacker said that he crossed paths with you in the kitchen that day. That you noticed him carrying a flask."

Bonnie chewed her lip. "I definitely remember the flask because it was so pretty. Usually the ones I see are silver, but his looked like it was made of gold or something."

Kit rolled her eyes. "Of course it was."

"Did you see him do anything with the flask? Pour the contents into a glass, maybe?"

Bonnie shook her head. "I saw him drink from it, which was odd because we were in his house and there were a billion glasses around."

Kit shook her head, confused. "Wait. You saw him drink from the flask?"

"Yes," Bonnie said. "Then his wife told him to slow down. That he was always drinking too much and making a mess of things."

Kit's eyes bulged. "His wife was with him?" So far, no one had implicated Pauline Pennypacker. In fact, she seemed to be the only Pennypacker not linked to the crime.

Bonnie nodded. "She told him it was important to be sober the entire time for Clara's sake and then they went back inside."

Kit cocked her head. "Inside? I thought you were in the kitchen."

"No. I saw him with his flask on the terrace when I was bringing out a tray of wine glasses."

"Wine glasses," Kit repeated.

"Yes, we served wine on the terrace during the cocktail hour and the reception. I assumed he had the flask to tide himself over until the bar officially opened. I mean, it was his house. I guess he could do whatever he wanted, really." She examined a purple nail. "Anyway, those glasses went like hotcakes. We couldn't keep them on the table. I spent most of my time running back and forth from the kitchen to the terrace." She held up the activity tracker on her wrist. "I logged twenty thousand steps that day."

"Great job." Kit inclined her head. "What about Steven Pennypacker, the brother? Did you notice him at all?"

Bonnie laughed. "I didn't see it myself, but one of the waiters said that Steven threatened to punch him when he accidentally bumped his arm with a tray of food. That guy's a real hothead."

"What's the waiter's name?"

"George Pickford. He moonlights for us, but mostly he waits tables at the Weston Inn." The Weston Inn was located in Liberty Square in the heart of Westdale. Kit knew it well because the Pilgrim Society's monthly meetings were held there.

"Well, well, well. Fancy seeing you here." At the sound of Harley's voice, Kit swallowed hard.

"Placing a last minute Christmas order?" Jamison asked.

Kit forced a smile. "Merry Christmas, guys. My mother loves the roast goose they prepare here."

Harley and Jamison exchanged glances. "Isn't Diane widely known as the best cook in Westdale?" Harley asked, referencing her mother's cook and housekeeper.

"Not when it comes to goose. That's Calliope Catering." She winked at the women behind the counter. "Right, ladies?" The two bobbed their heads in unison and Kit smacked a hand on the countertop. "Now that we've settled that, I'll see you both later."

As she attempted to walk between the young cops, they each blocked her with a shoulder.

"You weren't here to ask questions about Mitch's story, by any chance?" Jamison asked.

Kit silently cursed Mitch. He was supposed to reveal something that he hadn't told the police.

"You know perfectly well that you're not allowed to play detective," Harley added. "Romeo's explicit orders."

Kit pushed their shoulders aside. "Romeo is not the boss of me. I can do what I like."

"How very Winthrop of you," Jamison remarked.

Kit raised her chin a fraction. "If that's the way you want to look at it."

"It isn't," Harley said. "But you're not giving us much choice. Romeo said the next time we see you interfering in police business that we should arrest you." His gaze dropped to the floor and Kit knew that he didn't love the idea of arresting her.

She drew a deep breath. "Guys, I was checking on a goose. That's all. Now if you'll excuse me." She left the room in a hurry, afraid they'd see the tears in her eyes.

She made it safely inside her car before breaking down. She opened the glove compartment and pulled out spare napkins from Butter Beans. As she dabbed at her eyes, she tried to focus on the information she'd just acquired. Forget Romeo. If his idea of a girlfriend was someone who obeyed his every command, then he needed Siri, not Kit. He couldn't control her. No one could. Everyone who'd ever tried had failed and, if Romeo hadn't learned that by now, then he really didn't know her at all.

The Christmas Eve party at Greyabbey was more like a European circus than a stodgy Westdale affair. Heloise eschewed the bombastic tendencies of the Pennypackers — she'd never allow semi-clad fire-eaters, for example — but she liked to include things of visual interest. The garden area sported an ice sculpture of a trio of angels and a contortionist kept people's attention in the main reception room, along with the spider monkey-cum-trapeze artist.

Kit shoved another oatmeal raisin cookie in her mouth and washed it down with eggnog. So she'd gained a few pounds over the past month; she'd forgotten how good food could taste.

"Slow down or you'll be diabetic by morning," her mother warned.

Kit sniffed her glass. "What's in this eggnog?"

"Why? Worried it might be poison?"

Kit narrowed her eyes. "Not funny."

"Maybe a little funny."

"It's delicious, but it doesn't taste like Diane's recipe and I usually prefer her concoctions to anyone's."

"High praise indeed," her mother replied. "Truth be told, it's your grandmother's recipe. I found it in a cookbook when I was researching the menu for tonight and asked Diane to make it."

"Dad would've liked that," she said softly.

Heloise grunted a response before blending in with the guests.

"Kit, you look so pretty." Diane appeared behind her, carrying another tray of cookies. Kit fought the urge to grab another handful.

"Thanks."

"What are your plans for tomorrow? Anything special?"

"As I'm sure you already know, Mother's trying to get me to spend the night here, but I'm planning to go home."

"She wants you to wake up here on Christmas morning like old times," Diane said, understanding.

"Fat chance," Kit replied. "Don't you remember the last time I spent the night here for Christmas?"

Diane tapped her chin, thinking. "Not really."

"No, you wouldn't because you decided to visit your parents in Utah that year," Kit continued. "Huntley was in St. Kitts so it was just me. She made me do an emergency run for gin and rum in the middle of the night. No respectable place was open so I had to drive to some sketchy neighborhood in fear for my life. The worst part was, I wasn't even twenty-one. She gave me her driver's license to use."

Diane glanced at the near empty eggnog bowl. "Well, I know who to go to if my rum supply runs low tonight."

"Not on your life."

Diane lowered her voice. "I heard all the Pennypackers confessed."

"Not all. Just two."

"The two that like to hear the sound of their own voices."

Cecilia Musgrove approached them, her face pinched. "Season's Greetings, my lovelies. Where's that detective friend of yours, Kit? I want to ask him about the investigation. Isn't he usually attached to your hip?"

If only, Kit thought. "He's busy," was all she said. No need to fuel Cecilia's penchant for gossip.

Diane handed the Musgrove matron a glass of eggnog. "Just the way you like it."

"Thank you, my pet. I'm surprised you remember."

"You tell me every year," Diane said. "How can I forget?"

Kit promptly made her excuses and wandered from room to room, chatting with more Musgroves here and a few Winthrops there. She had a brief chat with Dr. Nina about her mother's menagerie. She was relieved when Francie and Charlotte finally appeared in the garden room. She crossed the room in a hurry and gave each girl a swift hug.

"Merry Christmas, Kit," Francie said. "Sorry we're late. Charlotte dropped her necklace down the sink and we had to call a plumber. Try finding a good one on Christmas Eve."

"I misjudged the clasp and then I couldn't catch it as it fell." Charlotte shrugged. She was accustomed to dropping, falling, and bumping into things with regularity and she had the bruises to prove it.

"You're here now," Kit said. "That's what counts."

Francie's eyes widened as she glanced over Kit's shoulder and out the window to the back garden. "Is that a wallaby wearing a Santa hat?"

"Don't ask," Kit said, taking a sip of eggnog.

"Still no Romeo?" Charlotte asked, her voice barely audible.

Kit shook her head. "He's still angry. So am I, for that matter."

"Is Crispin here?" Francie asked. "I didn't see him when we came in."

"Well, I think he's seen you," Kit said with a nod toward the doorway.

Crispin strode into the room. His blue eyes brightened when they fell upon Francie and he headed straight for the trio.

"Hey, Crispin," Kit greeted her cousin. "If you've come over here to talk me into New Year's Eve at the country club, you can forget it."

"Not at all," he said. "I came to tell Francie how lovely she looks this evening. And you, too, Charlotte."

Francie beamed.

"What about me?" Kit asked. If compliments were being distributed, she wanted one as well.

"I have something more important for you," Crispin said.

Kit felt a jolt of excitement. "Something about Betty Bitterbridge?"

Charlie raised his brows in exasperation. "No. It's about Charlie Owen."

Kit gripped his arm. "Please don't tell me you're publishing a review of his drivel. Do not give that man any more attention."

"I thought you'd want to know that he's doing a book signing this Saturday at the big bookshop in Eastdale. One of my staff alerted me to it. She's on his mailing list, apparently." Crispin was the owner and editor of the *Westdale Gazette.* Although his career choice was a disappointment to the Winthrop family, he managed to stay in their good graces. Unlike Kit.

"Thanks for letting me know," Kit said. She couldn't believe Charlie had the nerve to do a book signing in her own backyard.

"Bring your brawny boyfriend," Crispin suggested. "It would probably drive Charlie mad."

Kit's heart skipped a beat at the thought of Romeo. "I would, but he's not exactly in the picture."

"What? Why?"

"You heard him at the wedding. I'm pretty sure everyone did. He doesn't care for my Ellie Gold tendencies. He wants me to be a boring college student and nothing more."

"I doubt it's as simple as that," Crispin said.

"Maybe you haven't noticed, but Romeo's not a complicated guy. Kinda one of the reasons I like him." She sighed and swallowed the last of her eggnog.

"In that case, your mother must be pleased," he noted. Heloise was not a fan of the working class detective.

"Heloise doesn't do pleased."

Crispin knew that all too well. His aunt had been as annoyed as his parents when he'd opted for a career in journalism. She took every opportunity to remind him that he was working in a dead field.

"Do me a favor," Crispin said. "If you decide to go and cause a scene at the bookstore, could you at least give me a heads-up? I'd love to have someone cover it for the *Gazette*."

Kit snorted. "That would go over really well with our family. A bookstore brawl."

"Have it in the literary section," he advised. "It's classier."

"I'll take it under advisement."

"Is your sister here?" Francie asked.

"Arabella is skiing in the Alps, I'm afraid," Crispin replied.

"Why does she get to escape Mayflower madness?" Kit grumbled.

"She's in college," Crispin said.

"So am I," Kit exclaimed. Over Crispin's shoulder, she spotted Tom and Tip Bitterbridge as they entered the room.

Charlotte followed Kit's gaze. "Are you sure that's a good idea?"

Kit placed her empty glass on a passing waiter's tray. "They've lost Betty. It's our civic duty to help them."

"But not our job," Francie reminded her. "We're not professionals."

"Let her go," Crispin urged. "The more you tell her not to do something, the more she wants to do it."

Kit smiled at her cousin. They had that much in common.

"I'll be back," she promised and approached the Bitterbridge men on the far side of the room.

"Merry Christmas, Kit. You're looking well," Tip said, giving her a peck on the cheek.

"Thank you. I'm pleased to see you both here."

Tom's knuckles tightened around the pint of beer in his hand. "It was better than moping at home."

"Any news?" she asked quietly.

Tom gulped his beer. "The police said they're following up on all possible leads. I just wish they'd do it faster."

"I understand how you feel," she said, "but, unfortunately, the holidays slow everything down." She'd experienced that firsthand. When she'd called the Weston Inn to ask about George Pickford's schedule, they told her that he was out until Friday, so her impatient hands were tied until after Christmas.

Tip sighed. "At least your mother had the decency not to invite the Pennypackers."

"She wouldn't anyway," Kit admitted. "My parents were never fans of the Pennypackers." She glanced at Tom. "Sorry. I don't mean Clara. Clara's lovely."

Tom stared at the floor. "I don't know anymore."

"You two haven't reconciled?"

"How can they?" Tip asked. "Her family seems positively gleeful about the fact that they murdered my wife. Pauline is the only sensible one over there."

Kit gave the older man's arm a sympathetic squeeze. "I don't think they're gleeful, Mr. Bitterbridge. I think they're protecting their own, just like you would."

"Betty was a difficult woman, I know that." Tip's face reddened and Kit got the sense that he'd tossed back a few drinks before his arrival. "And God knows she had no love for the Pennypackers."

Tom shot his father an irritated look. "Excuse me. I'm going to say hello to Crispin."

Tip threw up his hands in despair. "Even my relationship with Tom is falling apart. Now is when we need each other the most."

"How have you been keeping your mind off things?"

"I'm in my study with a decent book, trying to pretend this whole mess never happened."

"I've spoken to Mitch," Kit confessed. "His information doesn't add up, though. I can't decide whether he's making false claims because he knows the real story or because he just wanted Clara off the hook."

Tip leaned closer, his interest piqued. "What kind of information?"

"He claims to have poisoned Betty's glass back in the kitchen before they were brought to the head table. None of the catering staff recalls seeing him in the kitchen. Bonnie, the one he said saw him, only saw him on the terrace, drinking out of the flask."

"The flask he claims to have dispensed the poison from?" Tip asked.

Kit nodded. "Pretty incredible, right? The police found no trace of poison in the flask but Mitch insists that he washed it out afterward and then filled it with whisky."

"Did he say what kind of poison he used?" Tip asked. "As far as I know, the police haven't received the toxicology report yet. If it's the same poison, it could prove that he really does know something."

Kit shook her head. "He apparently told the police that since he pays their salaries with his exorbitant taxes, they can figure it out themselves."

Tip looked lost in thought. "It's a relief that Clara takes after her mother."

"Are you convinced that Clara had no part in it?" Kit wasn't sure what Tip's thoughts were on the subject of Clara.

Tip sniffed. "I don't think so. Betty wouldn't have believed it, either. In fact, Betty would be the first one to admit that Clara wasn't capable of such a heinous crime."

"I thought Betty gave a wonderful speech," Kit said, wanting to say something positive about Betty. It was Christmas Eve, after all. "At the very least, the last memory people have of her is a nice one."

Tip chortled. "I was as surprised as anyone that she chose the path of least resistance. I was ready for her to offer scathing commentary on Pennypacker family history."

"It was out of character, wasn't it?" Kit said with a laugh.

"But you're right," Tip said. "It ended up being a good thing. Our marriage wasn't ideal…" He trailed off. "I'd wanted better for Tom. I thought he was so lucky, falling head over heels in love like that. I never had that."

Kit could see the emotion stirring in his soft brown eyes. "You didn't voice an objection to the marriage?"

"I certainly wasn't vocal about it. I knew it would be difficult for them," he admitted. "And that upset me more than anything. From the moment they got engaged, Betty was determined to break them up. Obsessed even. I couldn't have a conversation with her without hearing about her latest idea."

"They'd hidden their relationship until the engagement, hadn't they?" Kit had heard about their clandestine dating from Crispin.

He nodded. "They knew how their families would react."

"What do you think made Betty stop obsessing?" Kit asked.

Tip grabbed a glass of mulled wine from a passing waiter. "One day she just stopped talking about it. It was the day after Clara's bridal shower. I think she saw how happy Tom and Clara were together. She finally accepted that the wedding was inevitable and there was nothing she could do to stop it."

Kit remembered hearing about the bridal shower from Heloise. Betty had come to Greyabbey to vent afterward. Apparently, the shower had been 'a gauche spectacle.' Betty had been particularly put off by the shirtless men in bow ties who handed out cocktails with names like 'Dirty Bombshell' and 'Sex on the Beach.' It seemed that Betty had opted not to share her negative views with her husband.

"Tip, darling, so good of you to come." Heloise swept into the room to mingle with the guests in the garden room. She gave him a kiss on each cheek and wiped away the lipstick with her thumb.

"Merry Christmas, Heloise," he said. "Betty would have loved to be here."

"No doubt." She directed her gaze at Kit. "She lit up a room, that Betty."

More like darkened a doorstep, Kit thought.

"Did you know my Katherine is looking for a suitor?" Heloise asked.

"I most certainly am not," she said tersely.

"She'll have no trouble," Tip said. "No trouble at all. I heard the Breedloves are looking to make a match for one of their boys."

Kit swore under her breath. Not the stupid Breedloves again.

"It was nice chatting with you, Mr. Bitterbridge. Merry Christmas." She moved away before her mother could humiliate her any further. Then again, it wouldn't be a holiday at Greyabbey without a healthy dose of humiliation amidst empty bottles of alcohol.

Kit stumbled to her feet at the sound of the doorbell, fighting a thumping eggnog hangover. Who on earth would be on her doorstep on Christmas morning? She slid on her bunny slippers and padded downstairs. She'd managed to avoid getting roped into an overnight stay at Greyabbey. After several rounds of drinks, her mother was too busy entertaining guests with Dickens' tricks to notice Kit's departure. She opted to brave the cold rather than risk sharing her childhood bed with a python or a three-legged fancy rat so she trudged to Thornhill Road sometime after midnight. At least it was downhill.

"Romeo?" She blinked at the handsome man in a suit on her doorstep. "What are you doing here?"

He shoved his hands in his coat pockets and Kit could see that he was shivering. "I went to midnight mass and I haven't been able to sleep."

"Do you want to come in?" she asked. "It's freezing out there."

He shook his head. "If I come in, I'll want to stay."

"So stay." She didn't care that her hair was a bird's nest or that her feet were adorned with fluffy bunnies. It was Romeo and she missed him.

"Harley and Jamison said they saw you at Calliope Catering."

Uh oh.

"I was placing an order for Christmas dinner," she lied.

"Roast goose, right?" He raised an eyebrow and she knew he'd gotten the truth out of the catering staff.

"What about it?" she asked and heard the defensive tone in her voice.

"This is my fault, Kit. I take full responsibility. I never should have let you get involved in cases in the first place. I thought it was cute and a little bit sexy," he admitted. "But I never expected you to get so obsessed with solving murders."

"I'm not obsessed," she insisted. "Tom's a friend and he's miserable without his new wife. I want to see them reunited."

"I think you miss your old life and this is a way of rekindling it."

"If you're my old life, then yes, I absolutely miss it."

He winced. "Not me. I mean TV. Hollywood. The thrill of the hunt."

"But," she began and Romeo held up a hand to stop her.

"Please let me finish. It took me hours to work up the nerve to come here. The whole time I was supposed to be listening to the sermon, I was thinking about you."

Kit folded her arms across her chest. "Because I'm the devil you need to cast out."

"No, of course not," Romeo objected, dragging a frustrated hand through his hair. "Because you're Kit and I want to come inside. I want to be with you, but I can't. I'm not a good influence on you, putting you in danger all the time."

"Romeo, you're not making sense." She just wished he would come inside and wrap his strong arms around her. Tell her that it was all a big mistake.

"Trust me, Kit. I am. You need to move on with your life. Get your college degree. Stop getting involved with guys like Charlie Owen and me. Guys that you know you don't have a future with."

Anger coursed through Kit's veins. Who was he to decide that they had no future together?

"Charlie Owen? Why on earth are you lumping Charlie in a category with you? You're nothing alike." Kit took a step back, starting to piece together his mental process. "You kept reading his book, didn't you?" In the book, Charlie devoted an entire page to his theory on Kit's reasons for dating him, including pissing off her mother. Kit was furious when she'd read it and had closed the book, unwilling to continue reading anymore.

Romeo's guilty look was the only answer she needed.

"If you have questions about why I want to be with you, you should ask me," Kit said hotly.

"I haven't finished the book yet," he admitted. "I had to stop when..." He tightened his fists. "Let's just say I'm glad the guy's not local or I'd be risking probation."

Kit wondered which part of the book bothered Romeo the most, whether they'd stopped reading at similar places.

"Please back off the investigation," Romeo pleaded. "I'm not trying to put you in any preconceived box, I swear. I just couldn't bear it if anything happened to you. I'd never forgive myself."

"Romeo, you're making a mountain out of a molehill. The Pennypackers don't pose a threat to me."

"You don't know what they're capable of," he boomed. "If one of them was willing to kill a Bitterbridge, then why not you? Being a Winthrop Wilder won't protect you from guys like that. Guys who think they own the world."

Kit couldn't hide her disappointment. As much she'd hoped for a different outcome, his tune hadn't changed. He still believed that she couldn't take care of herself. That she was weak and helpless. Romeo and her mother had more in common than they knew.

"So this is the real reason you're here on Christmas," she said. "To tell me to back off for my own good. How patriarchal of you."

He shrugged. "I wanted to see you on Christmas. It's my day off."

"Well, it's mine, too," she said. "So I'm going to ask you to leave now. Merry Christmas, Romeo." Quickly, she closed the door so that he didn't see her burst into tears.

Chapter Four

Kit didn't stop her investigation. If anything, Romeo's little speech made her want to solve the murder even more. School was out until mid-January and she had plenty of free time. Her desire to solve the case had nothing to do with her old life. She wanted to help and she was good at it. Why couldn't Romeo see that?

The day after Christmas, she decided to pay a visit to Clara Pennypacker. Clara was still living in the home she'd been sharing with Tom on the outskirts of Westdale. Even though he'd returned to Oakheart, Clara had decided to stay and patiently await his return.

Kit knew from Tom that Clara liked to go for a morning run at the park near their house. Kit was sorely in need of exercise after her excessive holiday indulgences. It was a win-win.

She spotted Clara ahead of her in cobalt blue lululemon gear, her high ponytail swinging in the breeze. Kit increased her speed in an effort to catch up, but kept her footfall as ninja-like as possible. She didn't want Clara to think she was being chased, not after what happened to Betty.

"Clara?" she said, feigning surprise. "I didn't realize you were a runner."

Clara smiled. "Hi, Kit. I came late to it." Her breathing was labored. "I was determined to lose ten pounds before the wedding. Then I discovered that I actually liked running so I've kept it up."

"Good for you. It's a chore as far as I'm concerned, but a necessary one since I'm not giving up carbs in this lifetime."

"How are you holding up anyway?" Kit asked, keeping pace with her.

Clara rolled her eyes. "Not great. I belong to a family of murderers, after all."

"No one's been arrested. I guess that's good news."

"Not from Tom's point of view," Clara said. "Steven said to give him time, that he'll come around eventually."

"Steven was very brave, confessing like that. What did he tell the police? Was it something similar to your dad?"

"Pretty much. He said he poisoned Betty's champagne before she arrived at the reception."

"How did he know which glass was Betty's if she wasn't seated?"

Clara stared at the path ahead. "I sort of made the seating plan. My family saw it a hundred times on the dining room table."

"What do you mean 'sort of?"

"Let's not pretend that I had total control over every aspect of the wedding," she complained. "Even with her negative attitude, Betty insisted on getting involved and calling the shots."

Kit knew that Betty had possessed the control freak gene that plagued Heloise, too. "What about your mom?" she asked. "Did she get involved?"

Clara laughed and her frosty breath punctured the air. "My mother is a quiet woman. She leaves the talking to my dad." She hesitated. "She did get worked up a few times over Betty's antics, though. She even spoke to Tip Bitterbridge about it. That's how annoyed she was."

"Which antics in particular?"

Clara threw her hands in the air as she ran. "Pick one. I could hardly keep track. Betty was determined to make the whole affair difficult from beginning to end. Stuck her pointy nose in everything from the seating chart to the music to the menu. She insisted that the mother and son dance be to a song called *I Told You So* even though Tom and I had already chosen *Unforgettable.* I don't even know what the song is about, but I could tell from the title that she was trying to make a statement."

Kit didn't doubt it.

"She also instructed the catering staff to provide Krug Brut champagne and Beluga caviar and expected my family to foot the bill."

"What did your mother say?"

"She offered Cristal and salmon roe instead," Clara said. "Betty agreed to the Cristal but wouldn't hear of salmon roe. Thought it was embarrassing to offer the guests anything less than Beluga. Made some snide remark that maybe our bank account wasn't as robust as my father claimed."

"Is there a chance it isn't?"

Clara narrowed her eyes. "This wasn't about money. This was a power play. My whole family got fed up with Betty's petty antics."

And seemingly put an end to them. A permanent end.

"So where did Steven say he put the container that he used for the poison?" Kit asked, thinking of Mitch's flask claim that didn't pan out. "I understand the police searched the house and came up empty-handed."

"Well, he said he threw it away at the reception," she replied and cast a sidelong glance at Kit. "He already told the police all this."

"But they haven't found it."

She shrugged. "It's their job to come up with the evidence."

"True." That sounded like her family's lawyer talking.

"Have the police tracked the garbage from the reception?" she asked.

Clara wrinkled her nose at the mention of garbage. "I don't know."

"Well, did Steven say what kind of poison he used? Where he got it?"

"Have mercy, Kit. Are you working for your cousin now?" Clara asked, her porcelain cheeks flushed. "I feel like you're writing an article for the *Gazette*." She picked up the pace in effort to put distance between them.

"I just want to help, Clara," Kit called. "I want you and Tom to start your life together."

Clara stopped running and turned around, jogging in place. "Why?"

Kit blinked. "What do you mean?"

"Why do you want Tom and I together? You don't even know me. Your family never liked us. We've always been excluded from Winthrop and Wilder events."

"I like *you*," she said. "And Tom's a friend. I want to see him happy."

"Are you sure you don't have another angle?" Clara asked, her eyes narrowing.

"What other angle?"

"Who better to marry a Bitterbridge than a Winthrop Wilder?" she remarked. "That's what Betty kept whispering in my ear. That Tom deserved better than a dreadful Pennypacker. When you moved back to Westdale, she spoke of you nonstop. Every time I saw her. How beautiful you are. How smart you are to go back to college." She jerked an angry finger at herself. "I already have a college degree."

Kit was flabbergasted. "I've never had any romantic interest in Tom, I swear." She stopped running all together now, too thrown off guard to continue.

"Since when does actual romance matter when it comes to a Mayflower match?" Clara sucked water from her hydration kit. "I'm telling you, Betty had her eye on you for Tom. Ask your mother. I'm sure they discussed at length over Xanax and cocktails."

With that parting shot, Clara turned on her heel and ran away. Kit stood on the path, in complete shock. Her mother had pushed a Breedlove in her direction but never a Bitterbridge. And Betty appeared to have come to terms with Tom's marriage. Clara had to be mistaken. It had to be jealousy talking. But why be jealous of Kit when the man Clara loved had already married her?

Kit wiped the sweat from her brow. Never mind that it was the Christmas holidays. If she hoped to find Betty's killer, then she needed to roll up her sleeves and get her hands dirty. Clearly, she still had a lot of work to do.

"Mother, you came." Kit smiled at the sight of her mother on the front step of her house on Thornhill Road. Heloise generally only used the streets below Greyabbey as a route to downtown. For her, it was Winding Way or the highway.

"In the spirit of Christmas, it's time I see what you've done with the place," Heloise said, taking a hesitant step inside. She looked worried that she'd acquire the plague simply by standing in Kit's entryway.

"You'd need to lick the floor to risk catching anything," Kit advised, sensing her mother's discomfort.

Heloise glanced at her sharply and continued into the living room. "You kept the original flooring," she observed. "Very nice."

Heloise approved of all things preservation and conservation. She was active on every committee in Westdale.

"Gin?" Kit offered. Her mother's Kryptonite.

"Don't mind if I do." She trailed Kit into the kitchen. "What an adorable kitchenette."

Kit handed her mother a cucumber and gin that she'd prepared in advance. "It's not a kitchenette, Mother. It's an actual kitchen."

Heloise's critical gaze swept across the room. "How do you manage to cook anything in a space this small?"

"I manage fine," she snapped. It wasn't as though her mother had ever cooked a meal in her life. What did she know about the space required?

Kit poured herself a sparkling water. Normally she would have preferred to dull the memory of her mother's visit with alcohol, but she needed to be sharp for this particular conversation. This little tête-à-tête had a purpose.

"Have you met the new neighbors?" Heloise asked. "I understand they're ethnic."

Kit sighed in exasperation. "They're Hispanic, if that's what you mean, and they'll be a great addition to the neighborhood." Kit knew that, in Heloise's mind, anyone who wasn't a Mayflower descendant was ethnic.

"It's this house that's the problem," Heloise said, sipping her drink. "Because it was a foreclosure, now the property prices have dropped. Mark my words, the street will suffer."

Kit rolled her eyes. She couldn't understand how a woman so devoted to every animal under the sun could be so bigoted when it came to other human beings.

She moved back to the living room and sat down on the sofa while Heloise perched on the edge of a chair. "Why don't I lend you my interior decorator as a special Christmas treat?"

"No, thank you. That isn't necessary."

"You're planning to do the work yourself?" Heloise queried. "Over the holiday break?"

Kit fought to control her temper. "It isn't necessary because the work is done."

Heloise looked faintly surprised. "Oh, I see. Well, you always did favor that bohemian look."

"Tip seemed depressed at your party," Kit said, ready to get the ball rolling. She wasn't going to last an hour with her mother here or there'd be another homicide for Romeo to work. A murder-suicide, more likely.

"Can you blame him? He wants the murderer brought to justice, as do we all."

"The police still don't have enough evidence to arrest either one of the Pennypackers."

"That Mitchell Pennypacker is such a bore. They should arrest him simply for being an ass."

"Then half of Westdale would be under arrest."

"Only half?" Heloise raised a pencil-lined eyebrow.

"I heard they figured out what killed Betty," Kit lied. She needed to know whether Heloise was still getting updates on the case from Chief Riley. Without Romeo's inside information, Kit's options were limited.

"You mean aside from the massive heart attack, of course," Heloise said.

"Obviously."

"Who would have guessed coprine? I mean, my money was on arsenic, but the toxicology report was pretty conclusive."

Kit had no idea what coprine was, so she faked it. "Crazy, right?"

"There were mushrooms on the salad, but I can't believe the caterers would be foolish enough to use poisonous ones. It had to be deliberate."

Okay, so coprine was a poison found in mushrooms. "Otherwise, lots of people would've eaten them," Kit said in an effort to keep the conversation flowing.

"Exactly. So the killer must have known that there would be mushrooms in the salad. They could easily have added inky cap mushrooms to Betty's plate without her noticing. That could explain why the police haven't turned up a discarded vial or bottle. Maybe the killer had a pocketful of mushrooms."

Kit nodded, absorbing the new details. Coprine from inky cap mushrooms. "People seemed sure that it was something in her champagne, but I guess not."

Heloise tossed back the rest of her drink. "Goodness, no. Inky cap mushrooms liquefy into black goo. If black goo had been tipped into a champagne flute, Betty definitely would've noticed. It had to be mushrooms on the salad."

Kit didn't even remember the salad; she was too distracted by the memory of Betty's death and Romeo's sharp words.

"Betty was right about those Pennypackers, God rest her wealthy soul." Heloise seemed to be unfamiliar with the phrase *you can't take it with you.*

"Speaking of Betty," Kit began, "did she ever mention wanting to set me up with Tom?"

The cagey look in Heloise's eyes answered the question. "Perhaps on occasion."

"And what was your response to that?"

"We'd address it when the time was right."

Kit laughed. "When would the time have been right? Tom was getting married to Clara."

"Betty thought it might not last. Most marriages don't, you know. You're lucky to have parents who stayed together."

"Yes, but Dad died," Kit pointed out. "Divorce isn't an option when one of you is dead."

"Thank you for the reminder," Heloise said.

"Clara seemed to think that Betty had a plan to marry me off to Tom. In fact, she seemed pretty annoyed about it." Not that Kit blamed her.

Heloise shrugged. "Thanks to the Pennypackers, Betty is no longer here to make plans. That reminds me, I need to plan a few words in Betty's honor for the meeting tonight. You're coming, right?"

"With jingle bells on," Kit said brightly. No need for her mother to know that she had an ulterior motive. An ulterior motive named George Pickford.

"Excellent." Heloise held up her glass. "Now where is that housekeeper of yours? I can't be expected to sit here holding an empty glass, can I?"

Kit turned down the heat on her homemade tomato sauce to let it simmer. Before their fallout, Romeo had chastised her for buying sauce in a jar and had given her his mother's secret recipe. It confused Kit to no end that his family referred to sauce as 'gravy.' As far as she was concerned, gravy was poured on a roast, not on pasta.

The phone sprang to life and Kit recognized the ringtone for Beatrice Coleman, her agent in Los Angeles. She'd been so caught up with exams and the holidays that she hadn't spoken to Beatrice in weeks.

"Happy Hanukkah, Bea," Kit said.

"Hanukkah's come and gone, doll, but I'll take it. Thank you." She paused and Kit envisioned her taking a long drag of her cigarette. "How'd your exams go?"

"No results until January, but I feel pretty good about them."

"Excellent. Good for you. So listen, I've been meaning to talk to you about something."

Kit chuckled. "Let me guess. *Fool's Journey*?"

"Oh, you know about that, huh?"

"I'm in Pennsylvania, not Antarctica. We even have indoor plumbing."

"Are you upset?"

Kit stirred the pasta in the pot to keep it from sticking. "A heads-up would've been nice."

"I thought it might work in your favor if we rode it out. Have you Googled yourself lately? Your name is blowing up the internet."

Kit had been so busy lately that she hadn't engaged in her usual vanity routine. She'd barely posted on Twitter or Instagram, only a photo of her posing in front of the Christmas tree in Liberty Square. She wished her followers 'happy holidays' and never checked her stats.

"I haven't been online that much," Kit admitted.

"You're on a break from school now, hon," Beatrice said. "You should be promoting yourself anywhere and everywhere while you have the time."

Kit set down the slotted spoon. "I've been preoccupied. A woman was murdered here recently. At her son's wedding."

"Another murder?" Another drag of the cigarette. "I thought you said Westdale was a bubble of wealth and snobbery."

"That doesn't preclude murder."

"If you want to distract yourself from all that death, your former snuggle bear is going to be in your neck of the woods for a book signing. You should think about dropping by. It would make a great photo opp."

"As it happens, I already plan to attend." She turned off the boiling water with a flourish.

"Do you want me to tip anybody off?"

"My cousin gets first dibs. He's the one who told me about it."

"You should put me in touch with him. He sounds like my kind of guy." She coughed, a deep, hacking cough that made Kit wince.

"I'll let you know how it goes," Kit said.

"If you play your cards right, you won't have to. It'll show up in my news feed."

"Happy New Year, Beatrice."

"Let's hope."

No sooner had Kit put a plate of steaming pasta on the table than the doorbell rang.

"It's Grand Central today," Kit muttered, hurrying to the front door. She opened the door to reveal Phyllis and Thora, wearing matching Santa hats and ringing bells. Both hats had the word 'Single' written in green glitter across the front.

"I saw you were making pasta," Thora said. "Can we come in?"

Kit's brow wrinkled. "The kitchen is at the back of the house. How could you see what I was making?"

Phyllis elbowed Thora. "Good job."

"I may have peeked through the back window," Thora confessed. "I saw the light on."

Kit threw her head back and sighed. "Come on in, ladies. Or should I say 'eligible elves.'"

She walked back to the kitchen and retrieved two more plates from the cupboard.

"This looks delicious," Thora said, sitting down in front of Kit's plate.

"Gee, would you like wine with that?" Kit asked sarcastically.

Thora clapped her hands together. "That would be perfect. Do you have any chianti? I like a good chianti with Italian food."

Phyllis joined her friend at the table. "Me, too. None of that California stuff."

Kit was glad she'd gone overboard on the pasta. "So when did you get back, Thora? I thought you'd stay with your daughter until after New Year's Day."

"I was meant to, but there were toys everywhere. I kept tripping over them. A place like that isn't safe for an old broad like me."

"Thora and I have decided to ring in the new year together this year," Phyllis said.

Kit poured the wine and then sat down at the table to eat. "Enjoy."

"I have to admit, when I saw you making pasta and homemade sauce, I hoped you might have company," Thora said.

Kit knew that she meant Romeo. Thora had a thing for the man she'd dubbed the Italian Stallion.

"Afraid not. I just need to eat early because I'm going to the Pilgrim Society meeting tonight."

Thora sipped her wine. "Early suits me. Then I can justify a late night snack."

"Have you spoken to Romeo since the wedding?" Phyllis asked.

Kit pictured him on the doorstep on Christmas, refusing to come inside, and her throat tightened. "Briefly."

"So what are you going to do about it?" Thora asked.

Kit swallowed a forkful of pasta. "Do?"

Thora polished off her wine like it was Mylanta. "You're a woman of action, Kit. So act."

"That's the problem. He wants me to be inactive. No sleuthing."

"Any new leads?" Phyllis asked. "My money's on the brother."

"I'll take that action," Thora said. "How much?"

"Five Andrew Jacksons," Phyllis replied.

Kit paused. "Why don't you just say one Benjamin?"

Phyllis narrowed her eyes. "You choose your favorite face and I'll choose mine. Jackson has a rugged handsomeness that appeals to me. Like Gregory Peck."

"Why is your money on Steven?" Kit asked.

"I've seen him throwing tantrums at the Westdale Country Club," Phyllis told her. "The guy has a temper."

"And he's very protective of his younger sister," Thora added. "Adelaide said that she once saw Steven pummel a kid for calling Clara a cry baby."

"A cry baby? How old was he?" Kit asked.

"Twelve," Phyllis answered.

Kit pressed her lips together. "That's some hard evidence."

"He has a penchant for throwing his racquet at his opponent when he loses a match," Phyllis added.

"I thought he played rugby and cricket," Kit said.

"He plays everything," Phyllis said. "That's what happens when your family is filthy rich and eager for everyone to know it."

"What do you think of Mitch?" Kit asked.

Phyllis chewed, considering the question carefully. "Pompous, brash…"

"Killer?" Kit prodded.

Phyllis shrugged. "Maybe. If he feels threatened."

"If his wallet feels threatened," Thora added.

"How did Betty Bitterbridge threaten him or his wallet?" Kit mused. "They both have more money than they could ever spend in their lifetimes."

"You need to make him jealous," Thora said.

Kit's brow furrowed. "Mitch Pennypacker?"

"No, Romeo," Thora said as sauce dribbled down her chin. She wiped it away with her forearm. "Didn't your mother's housekeeper teach you to put out napkins for your guests?"

Kit hopped up to grab paper towels. "To be fair, I didn't actually plan on having guests." She handed one paper towel to Thora and another to Phyllis.

"What about dating one of those cute cops?" Phyllis suggested. "They're young and pliable." She smiled dreamily.

"Harley and Jamison?" Kit asked, aghast. "Not going to happen."

"There must be someone to bring out the primal beast in him," Thora said.

Kit shook her head vehemently. "This is not high school. I'm not going to use some poor sap to make Romeo jealous."

"Too bad that Charlie Owen isn't here," Phyllis said. "I read what he said about you in his book." She fanned herself. "That would be enough to get Romeo's blood boiling."

Kit's fork hovered in mid-air. "You read the book?" She really needed to finish reading that stupid book before the book signing. Her time was nearly up.

"Of course," Thora said. "Our book club chose it for the book of the month. We're meeting tomorrow night if you want to come. It's my turn to host."

Kit rolled her eyes skyward. "You're in a book club? Where you actually read books?"

Thora and Phyllis exchanged glances. "We usually read erotic romance, but we made an exception for you."

Kit shuddered at the thought of a group of elderly women discussing passages with strong sexual content.

"You know, he's signing books in Eastdale tomorrow," she told them. She enjoyed the idea of Thora and Phyllis sexually harassing Charlie Owen.

"Really?" Phyllis took a thoughtful sip of wine.

"Why didn't you say so?" Thora asked. "That's your perfect chance. That's how you win Romeo back."

"Somehow, I don't think a photo of me yelling at Charlie in a bookstore is going to make Romeo come crawling back. I was making a plan for humiliation, not seduction."

"Humiliation is overrated. Wear that tight black sweater and pick us up at ten," Thora ordered.

"I'll do no such thing," Kit replied. "Revenge is not a team sport." *Unless you're a Pennypacker.*

No way would she reveal what time she planned to go. She knew they'd go early because neither one liked to drive in the dark. Kit thought it best to wait until the end of the day anyway when the crowd would be thinner.

"Maybe Pauline can update you on the case tomorrow night," Phyllis remarked, "since you don't have Romeo's ear."

"Or she could just show up at Romeo's in that black silk nightgown and interrogate the hell out of him," Thora said.

Kit opened her mouth to speak, not sure which comment to target first. She opted for Thora's.

"Okay, how do you know I have a black silk nightgown?"

"You posted a selfie on Instagram," Thora said. "If you don't want people to know you own one, don't take photos of yourself wearing it."

Kit sighed. "Why are you following me on Instagram? I live next door to you."

"We're being supportive."

"More like nosy," Kit said. She eyed Phyllis. "Your turn. Why would Pauline Pennypacker update me on the case tomorrow?"

"Because she's in our book group."

Kit slapped her forehead. "And you've only thought to mention it now?"

"We only meet once a month," Phyllis objected. "It's not like we knew there'd be a murder at her daughter's wedding."

"What time is book club?" Kit asked, a determined look on her face. Tomorrow was shaping up to be a busy day.

"Seven. Why?"

She adjusted her top. "Because you're going to have a special guest."

The Weston Inn was teeming with the paragons of Westdale society. Naturally, Betty's death was on everyone's lips tonight, from the bartender to the valet to the guests. Kit was relieved to see that no Bitterbridges were in attendance. She didn't want to risk being overheard asking too many questions about the investigation. She'd drawn Romeo's ire and sufficiently annoyed Clara. She didn't need to be in anyone else's doghouse.

"Kit, you're here for another meeting," Crispin exclaimed, stepping out from the shadows. "I thought for sure the novelty would have worn off by now."

"I'm not here for the novelty," she said. She looked around to see if anyone was listening. "I'm here to speak to a waiter named George about Steven Pennypacker."

Crispin grinned and patted her on the back. "We really are blood relatives, aren't we?"

"You, too?" she asked.

He nodded. "I got a tip that a waiter had an incident with Steven at the wedding. I was going to include it in the *Gazette* article about the ongoing investigation."

"Have the Pennypackers given you a hard time about printing the stories?"

He shook his head. "Are you kidding? They thrive on the attention. They're my dream subjects. Of course, Steven won't be forthcoming about the waiter. When I called and asked him about it, he told me to crawl back under Plymouth Rock."

"He's delightful," Kit said wryly.

"Do you have a description of George?" Crispin asked.

"Five feet, nine inches tall. Brown hair."

"I hope you're describing yourself," a deep voice rumbled.

Kit froze.

"Nice to see you, Romeo," Crispin said, confirming Kit's fears.

"I thought you didn't like these events," Romeo said to Kit.

"I don't like the dentist either, but I still go every six months," she countered.

"Kit." His gaze moved down the length of her and he sighed. "You look beautiful."

She cleared her throat, trying not to feel how much she missed him. "What are you doing here, Romeo? This is a closed event."

"Why do I get the sense that you already know why I'm here?" He studied her intently. "In fact, why do I get the sense that you're here for the same reason?" His jaw tensed.

"But that can't be, because Kit Wilder knows that she is not to involve herself in police business."

"She's not involving herself in police business," Crispin said. "She's doing *Westdale Gazette* business."

Kit played along without missing a beat. "That's right. I'm helping my cousin investigate this story."

"It's for college," Crispin clarified.

"I thought you were a psychology major," Romeo said.

"I am, but Westdale College is a liberal arts school. They want us to be well-rounded."

Romeo looked unconvinced.

"So she's interning with me over the holiday break," Crispin said. "I asked her to come tonight because I need to interview a waiter. I thought he'd be more inclined to open up to the famous Kit Wilder than to me."

Romeo looked from Crispin to Kit, deciding. "Fine," he said. "In that case, we'll speak to George together."

Kit's body relaxed and she mouthed a silent thank you to Crispin. He only nodded in response.

"Oh, look. I see the mayor by the bar," Crispin said. "I need to have a word with her about the parking meters on our street."

He hurried off without a backward glance and Kit knew that he was making himself scarce so that she had a few quiet minutes with Romeo. Crispin was easily the best of the Winthrops.

"So you've found a way to keep your nose both clean and dirty at the same time," Romeo mused. "I should have known better than to think you'd just stay out of it."

Kit reached for his hand, threading her fingers through his. "I miss you, Romeo. Do you think we can try to work through this?"

Gently, he closed his eyes and Kit could see that he was struggling to maintain his cool exterior. "I don't want to have the same arguments time after time. I don't like fighting with you and I definitely don't want to involve you in dangerous situations." He released her hand and shoved his own in his pocket. "I'm sorry, Kit."

"You won't," she insisted. "I'm a big girl and I make my own choices."

She ignored the lump in her throat and soldiered on. She couldn't let him see how much he'd hurt her. She spotted the waiter weaving his way through the sea of Lily Pulitzer and CK Bradley bodies. With his acne-marked skin and slicked back hair, George didn't look a day over sixteen.

"Look, I think that's him," she said, grateful for the distraction.

"Let's see if you can get him to talk, Lois Lane." Romeo winked, but there was no warmth in it.

Kit fluffed her hair and made a beeline for the gangly waiter. "Hello, George," she said, linking her arm through his free one. "Take a walk with me, would you?"

George stammered and stuttered his way out the back door. "Kit Wilder."

"And this is Detective Romeo Moretti." She jerked her thumb at the handsome man trailing them. "We'd like to ask you a few questions about the Pennypacker wedding."

He looked so startled that Romeo removed the tray of snacks from his hand, afraid that he'd drop it.

"It's okay," Kit said, touching his arm in an attempt to calm his nerves. "You're not in trouble. We just want to talk."

"I'm not in trouble?" he asked in a way that made Kit wonder what he thought he'd be in trouble for.

Romeo must have had the same thought because he uttered a vague, general statement. "Not if you tell us what you know."

"I only took one quick video," George said, his eyes pleading with Kit. "I uploaded it to Snapchat, not YouTube or anywhere else."

"Is it on your phone?" Kit asked, not sure what video he meant.

He nodded and retrieved his phone from his pocket. "I'll delete it right now if you want. I'm sorry. It won't happen again."

Romeo peered over her shoulder as Kit tapped open a video. The video was shot from above the table on an angle. An angle that gave a generous peek at a young woman's cleavage. Kit recognized the golden fabric of the dress that she wore to the wedding. Unfortunately for George, so did Romeo.

"You could get fired for this," Romeo boomed, swiping the phone from Kit's hand. He held the phone close to George's nose, threatening to crush it.

"I said I'd delete it." George's lip trembled and he looked close to tears.

"How did you manage to take this without anyone at the table noticing?" she asked.

He almost said, "I do it all the time." Instead, he offered, "It wasn't just me. I saw another dude there doing the same thing. I recognized him from school. Computer geek."

"Another waiter?" Romeo growled.

George shook his head violently. "No, a guest. Rich kid." He snapped his fingers. "Leonard Wallingford."

Kit gave Romeo a hard look. "We have more important things to worry about than a video of my boobs. Let it go." She turned back to George. "We'd like to ask you about the incident with Steven Pennypacker."

The color returned to his face and he appeared visibly relieved. "Oh, that."

"Yes, that." Romeo loomed over him and Kit could tell that George was still feeling under threat. Gently, she placed a hand on Romeo's arm.

"He said I bumped into him on purpose," George said. "Started yelling at me in front of everyone."

"Did he get violent?" Romeo asked.

"If he had, I probably wouldn't be standing here right now. He's a big guy." George braved another look at Romeo. "Not as big as you, but big enough to make me disappear into an empty room to use my inhaler." He patted his pocket. "I keep it with me at all times."

"Asthma?" Kit asked sympathetically. Her friend Jordan had been asthmatic as a child and had told her many embarrassing tales that he'd categorized as *things that impacted my cool factor*.

George nodded. "Of course, the room wasn't even empty. The place was crawling with Pennypackers, which I guess makes sense since it was their house."

"Which Pennypacker was in the room?" Romeo inquired.

"The mother. She was arguing with the groom's dad, Mr. Bitterbridge."

Kit cast a quizzical glance at Romeo, who looked as surprised as she did. "Wait. You witnessed an argument between Tip Bitterbridge and Pauline Pennypacker?"

"They weren't being loud, like shouting or anything, but I could tell they were arguing."

"How could you tell?" Kit asked.

George gave her a grim smile. "I have divorced parents. I know what quiet arguing looks like."

"Could you hear what they were arguing about?" Romeo asked.

George shook his head. "Didn't want them to see me. I got out of there fast and sucked the life out of my inhaler."

Wordlessly, Romeo deleted the video before handing the phone back to George. "Delete this from your account, too. I don't want to see this popping up anywhere. If I do, I'll come and find you and, trust me, your inhaler won't be able to save you."

George gulped. "I will. I swear."

"And if I ever see you with your phone out at an event again," Kit threatened, "I'll make a video of my own. You'll be the star." She smiled. "And it will be your worst nightmare."

Chapter Five

Charlie Owen sat at a long table, signing copies of his book. For the past few hours he'd been scribbling his name in each book presented to him, only looking up long enough to gauge the attractiveness of the fan. Truth be told, he was bored. His agent said that the book would be a good way to optimize his celebrity, but he was no longer sure it was worth his time, especially the grueling book tour. Podunk city after podunk town. Exactly how many women had Tory Burch bags anyway? He found himself doodling the logo between signings.

An elegant hand with plum polished nails produced a book. Another Tory Burch bag holder, presumably.

"To?" Charlie asked, without glancing up.

"The love of your life, of course."

Charlie started to scribble automatically until the words sank in. He jerked his head up to see Kit Wilder, even more beautiful than the last time he'd seen her. Her last day on the set of *Fool's Gold*. He'd been relieved then.

"Hello, old chum," she said, smiling. Or possibly gritting her teeth. He couldn't tell which.

"Chum." He tapped the pen against his chin. "Interesting choice of words." He saw the flash of a bulb out of the corner of his eye. Great, the press was on hand to capture the uncomfortable reunion.

"Dear Charles. Still so literal. Why don't you leave that to all these dusty books that nobody will actually read?"

He leaned back in his chair to study her. "Dear Kit, still vacuous. Why don't you leave that to all those professional actors?"

Kit smiled sweetly, unfazed. "You do realize you've just insulted yourself."

Charlie's ruggedly handsome face shifted from smug to confused. Kit noted that it was more expression than he usually managed to convey in a scene.

She took back her book, pretending to examine it. "So, surrounding yourself with books. Writing about other people's lives like mine. Too afraid to live your own?"

"Maybe you haven't noticed, but this line happens to be for people who are fans of my work."

"What *am* I doing here?" she asked in mock embarrassment.

"I would think you of all people would know the answer to that," he commented wryly. "Aren't you a college student now? Wouldn't want your ignorance to be showing." He smiled archly.

She straightened herself. "I've always been told that ignorance is bliss. At least that's what it's like for the women who date you."

The elderly woman behind Kit tapped her on the shoulder with a cane. "Pardon me, but would you mind moving things along? My arthritis is acting up and I do need to sit down."

"Certainly." She turned back to Charlie, smirking. "I'll leave you to your groupies."

Kit took her copy of the book and moved away from the table. Charlie tried not to watch her go but found that he couldn't stop himself.

Half an hour later, an exhausted Charlie walked back toward the restroom. He passed Kit sitting in a private nook, typing a text message on her phone. His book rested on the table beside her.

"You realize you're in a bookstore. You could at least make an effort." He removed the phone from her hands and placed it onto the table. She said nothing.

"Could you at least pretend to read my book while you're here?"

"I've already read your book, Charles. Cover to cover."

Charlie raised an eyebrow. "Let me guess. You've brought your bossy red pen and you're here to correct my grammar."

"I'll leave the heavy lifting to your editors."

"So what are you doing here?" he asked. "Hang on, am I near Pilgrim Town?" During their time together, Charlie had heard many stories about Kit's Mayflower-influenced hometown. It had sounded very different from his own Midwestern upbringing.

"As a matter of fact, I'm shooting a movie here over the holidays." The lie fell smoothly from her red lips. Charlie took the seat beside her, intrigued. "What's the film?"

"A period drama."

"Which period?"

Kit's eyes glazed over. "You know, an old period of history where people wore funny clothes and had old-timey haircuts."

He chuckled and patted her knee. "I have missed you, my Kit."

She jerked her leg away. "Don't patronize me, Chuck. I'm not your Kit anymore."

He looked into her eyes and sighed. "I do miss you on the set. Talia isn't nearly as fun as you were. I know you must miss me, too."

She stared at the table like a petulant child. "You didn't even come to see me after they fired me. I thought you would."

He rubbed a hand over his face. "And naturally you've been angry with me ever since."

"Of course I'm angry." Her cheeks grew flushed and she drew away from him. "You and Jordan were like my family. They exiled me and you didn't even call to see how I was. You didn't say anything."

Charlie knew perfectly well that he didn't reach out to her. And he knew perfectly well why.

"I'm sorry about that," he said. "But isn't that all ancient history? You can't be angry forever. You'll get frown lines." He leaned forward. "Say, when's the last time you had a facial?"

She pushed his forehead back with the heel of her hand. "I most certainly can be angry forever. I'm planning on a life of immortality just to achieve that goal."

He couldn't help but laugh. Kit wasn't a dramatic performer for nothing. It was the right thing for her and *Fool's Gold* had proved it. The show was a huge hit and Kit became a star. Bright and shining but, now, very much out of his reach.

"Did you really read the book?" he asked.

She nodded and stood to go. "It was good to see you, Charlie."

He'd forgotten how beautiful she was. The luxurious brown hair. The innocent yet alluring eyes. No wonder the face had found its way onto American television screens.

"How long are you filming here?" he asked, gathering his wits.

"Another couple of days," she lied.

"Would you like to get a drink?"

"Now? Aren't you bone tired?"

"I noticed a place around the corner. Had a picture of a fox and a hound on the sign. I'll meet you there in five minutes."

He headed swiftly toward the restroom before he could change his mind. He wasn't sure it was a good idea, but he didn't want to talk himself out of it. He'd been ducking Kit Wilder for a long time and, seeing her now, he wasn't sure that he wanted to duck anymore.

She was waiting for him when he arrived. She stood by the bar, wearing a V-neck black sweater and tight grey pants. Charlie tried not to notice how well the clothes suited her. He approached uneasily, as though she may bite. It wouldn't be the first time. She held a glass to her lips and he recognized the liquid gold inside.

"Bit early, isn't it?" he asked.

"Not judging by the way you look." She motioned to the bartender. "Two more whiskies, please."

Charlie cleared his throat nervously.

"What's the matter, Chuck? Whisky too manly for you?"

Charlie felt his tension fade. Kit had that effect on him, although he didn't like to admit it. "We'll start with your drink, princess."

They eyed each other competitively. The glasses were barely in front of them before they picked up their respective drinks and swallowed them. The bartender could barely contain his surprise.

"You're a bartender," Kit pointed out. "How is this image shocking?"

The bartender shook his head. "It's not every day I get the stars of *Fool's Gold* in my place trying to outdrink each other."

Charlie smiled sweetly. "Two glasses of your best sherry, please."

"Sherry? Are you channeling your inner grandmother?" Kit gave him a sidelong glance.

"I thought we should have something that's meant to be sipped. Pace ourselves."

Kit sensed the movement around them and knew that customers were taking their photo with whatever device was handy -- phone, iPad, and actual camera. She recognized the photographer from the *Westdale Gazette* who must have followed them from the bookstore. Kit had to play it cool. If Romeo ended up seeing the pictures, she had to appear oblivious to the attention or he'd accuse her of wanting her old life back again. She put all of her focus on Charlie.

Once the bartender delivered their latest round of drinks, she sauntered over to a vacant pool table.

"We're actually going to play pool?" he asked.

"Afraid you'll break a nail?"

"I would think you'd be more interested in throwing the balls at my head."

"The thought did occur to me."

He leaned his hip against the pool table. "Don't you want to know why I wrote about you in the book?"

Kit continued to set up the table. "Charlie, the truth is, I don't really care why."

Charlie stood still, momentarily stunned by her admission. "By all means, saddle 'em up."

"You mean rack 'em."

"Tomato, tom-ah-to."

Kit handed him a cue stick. "You break."

"And here I thought you were the ballbreaker."

He took his shot and the balls scattered. Nothing in the pockets.

"Someone nearly killed me earlier today," he said as she took her shot. "I had to call store security."

"Was she married to you?"

He smirked. "Not unless I was married to a bag of bones. She couldn't have been younger than eighty or more than ninety pounds but, man, she packed a wallop." He rubbed his chin, remembering.

"Sounds like someone I know." Now it was her turn to smirk. "So why do you think anyone would want to kill a famous guy like you?"

Charlie managed to sink two balls at once. "Pick a reason and you're probably right."

"Well, you've made off-the-cuff remarks about every minority group on the planet and you've banged more than your share of married women, including the wife of a prominent director." Kit managed to shoot two balls into the same pocket. "You also spent your first few years in Los Angeles in the company of unsavory characters just so you could get a feel for them." She glanced at him, feeling his eyes on her. "I told you I read your book."

He blushed slightly, embarrassed for only seeing her as a pretty face. She'd always been more than that. He'd only pretended not to notice. He leaned across the table to take his next shot. Kit averted her gaze, unwilling to acknowledge the long stretch of his body. She tried to think of Romeo, but that only made it worse.

"Your form's a bit off," she said, struggling to regain her focus.

He leaned on his cue and faced her.

"Maybe it's because my body responds too easily to irritation."

"Sounds like something you need to work on."

He took another shot and sank a solid ball.

"What do you know?" she said. "Your game could improve yet."

His next shot missed. Kit smiled smugly as she easily knocked in her striped ball. As she lined up for her next shot, she caught sight of Charlie juggling pool balls. She pulled herself up and placed a hand on her hip.

"Do you mind?"

"Not at all," he said pleasantly. "You don't distract me in the least. I'm a very focused juggler."

"Charlie, focus on something worthwhile. Your life, perhaps."

"How about we focus on your life for a second?" he countered. "Are you going to keep lying to me or have you decided to come clean?"

Kit's expression softened. He was an idiot, but he was an idiot with a good memory.

"You're not here shooting a film, are you?"

"Of course not," she said with a sigh. "You know I'm blacklisted."

"So wait? We *are* near Pilgrim Town?"

"Westdale and, yes, we are." Kit took her shot and sank the last striped ball. Then she sank the eight ball. Charlie watched in admiration.

"Is there anything you're not good at?"

"If there is, I'm sure you'll be the first to tell me about it."

His chest tightened at the harsh words. He had treated her cruelly and he knew it. He hoped the book helped Kit's opinion of him. It mattered to him, despite appearances.

"What if we made up for lost time?" he suggested. "Spend a little quality time together."

"I thought that's what we were doing," she replied, gesturing to the pool table.

He moved closer to her. "How long can you put up with me?"

"Don't you have a book tour to do?"

He shrugged. "Let me worry about that."

She checked her watch and smiled. "Okay, then. How would you feel about attending your first book club meeting?"

Kit heard the sounds of raucous laughter as she lifted her hand to knock on Thora's front door.

"Are you sure there's a book club meeting in there?" Charlie asked. "Sounds more like the lighting crew in a strip club."

Kit smiled to herself. "There are certain similarities."

"There's no red carpet. Just come in," Thora's raspy voice called and Kit opened the front door.

The book club members were gathered at the back of the house, seated around the informal dining table.

"Hold on to your Depends, ladies," Thora said. "Kit has brought us a holiday treat."

"Charlie Owen," one of the women exclaimed. Her fingers flew to her white hair, smoothing wayward tendrils.

He gave the group a casual wave. "Nice to be here, ladies." He twitched when he noticed Thora. "Hey, you're the lady who punched me."

Thora's eyes widened. "You must have me confused with some other old lady. That's discrimination, I tell you." She shook her head in disgust. "Why don't you just come out and say that we all look alike?"

As Charlie opened his mouth to respond, Kit gave a shake of her head. *Do not engage*, the shake said.

"So what's on the menu tonight, ladies?" he asked, rubbing his hands together eagerly.

Kit watched with amused interest as his gaze took in the empty shot glasses on the table. She could tell from his expression that he was wondering what he'd gotten himself into.

Thora padded into the kitchen. "What can I get you to drink? How about tequila with fennel bitters and a twist of lime?"

"You really did read my book," he said and Kit noted the pleasure in his voice.

"Well, we bought it for the pictures of you half naked," Thora admitted, "but the story was pretty good, too. I especially like the part where you talk about Kit's obsession with pancakes."

Charlie chuckled. "I had intimate knowledge of every diner in the L.A. area."

"How intimate?" Thora pressed him.

"Show us your scar," Adelaide piped up from the table. Her metal crutches rested against the wall behind her.

Kit suppressed a laugh. She knew exactly which scar Adelaide meant because she was the one who'd given it to him.

"That's Adelaide," Thora said. "I'm Thora. At the end of the table is Phyllis, next to her is Pauline, then Bernice. Lulu is in France for the holidays."

"Who needs to go to France for wine and cheese when you can buy it right here in Westdale?" Adelaide griped.

"Technically," Pauline said, "you'd need to go to Eastdale for the wine."

Adelaide shot her a nasty look. "The Pennypackers are all about technicalities these days, aren't they?"

Pauline reddened and Charlie saved the day by leaning over the table.

"Don't you need to take off your shirt?" Thora asked.

Charlie craned his neck to look at her. "The scar is here." He pointed to a tiny scar near his temple.

"Don't you have any on your back?" Phyllis asked. "I'll show you mine if you show me yours."

Charlie could see the writing on the wall. He pulled his top over his head and handed it to Kit.

"Ooh, it must be like old times for you two," Bernice enthused.

Charlie gave her a charming smile. "If it were like old times, the shirt would be ripped in half and I'd have a welt on my cheek."

"Charlie," Kit exclaimed, horrified. "You make it sound like I abused you."

He winked at her. "In all the right ways, honey."

Thora grabbed a bowl of potato chips and set it on the table. "Keep going. This is getting interesting."

Charlie turned his back to the ladies. "There's one below my shoulder blade. That was when I decided to stop doing my own stunts."

"Baby," Kit scoffed. She unbuttoned her trousers and showed off a larger scar on her hip.

"I remember that one," he said, admiring it. "The end of season one."

"Didn't stop me from doing stunt work," she said pointedly.

Thora stepped between them and rolled down the elastic waistband of her blue trousers. "Hip surgery," she said proudly. As she moved to drop her trousers further, Kit reached out a hand to stop her.

"Hey now, this is a PG event," Kit said.

Thora blinked. "But I have a scar from my C-section to show you."

Kit shook her head. "I think we've seen enough."

"Don't worry," Thora shot back. "I'm groomed."

Kit closed her eyes, willing the image out of her mind.

Phyllis stood and lifted up her blouse. "Appendectomy." Then she pulled down her own waistband. "Also hip surgery."

Charlie seemed to take the exhibitionists in stride. Kit suspected it wasn't the first time that older women voluntarily flashed their bits at him.

Bernice smiled shyly before standing and raising her reindeer sweater. "Boob job," she said, lifting the underwire of her bra. "My first husband asked me to get them, but I kept them in the divorce."

"Nice work," Charlie said and Bernice dropped back into her seat, exhilarated.

"What about you, Adelaide?" Kit asked. "You must have some impressive scars." She nodded toward the metal crutches. Anyone who needed help to walk surely had visual reminders.

"I'm not a braggart," she snapped. "I'll leave that nonsense to the rest of you."

Kit wondered if Adelaide's icy exterior would ever thaw. Looking at her tight, unpleasant expression now, she highly doubted it.

All eyes moved to Pauline who simply shrugged. "No scars, sorry."

"She is younger than the rest of us," Bernice pointed out.

"Kit's even younger and she has scars," Phyllis said.

"Kit puts herself out there," Pauline countered. "I don't do that. I'm more of a wallflower."

Kit thought that was probably a requirement when married to someone as brash as Mitch Pennypacker.

"Doesn't sound like you were a wallflower when you argued with Tip Bitterbridge at the wedding," Kit said quietly. "Takes a lot of guts to stand up to a Bitterbridge."

"How do you know about that?" she asked, her voice soft but guarded.

"Someone overheard you." Kit wasn't about to throw George under the bus.

Pauline grew flushed. "It was my daughter's wedding. I wanted it to be perfect."

"Well, I think we can all agree that you failed miserably," Adelaide said. "A dead mother of the groom, a suspicious bride and two confessions. Not exactly anybody's idea of perfect."

Tears glistened in Pauline's eyes and Thora shot Adelaide a warning glance. "You're not anybody's idea of perfect either, so zip it."

"I know how it looks, but Mitch and Steven wouldn't kill anyone," Pauline insisted.

"Who confesses to a crime they didn't commit?" Adelaide asked.

Pauline stared at the table, unwilling to discuss it. "I thought it might be a mistake to come tonight."

"The only mistake was the fact that I let Adelaide slither in here," Thora said. "You're in good company, Pauline." She glanced sharply at Adelaide. "Mostly."

"What did you and Tip argue about at the wedding?" Phyllis asked. "Tip's usually a reasonable man. Balanced out his wife."

At the mention of the deceased Betty Bitterbridge, Bernice made the sign of the cross.

Pauline pursed her lips, hesitant to answer. "I was unhappy about something that happened with Betty and I told Tip as much."

"Why Tip?" Kit asked.

"He was the best way to deal with Betty," Pauline admitted. "I'd tell him the latest problem and he'd tried to fix it. There was a lot of that in the months leading up to the wedding."

"I don't doubt it," Kit said.

"The seating plan was something I thought we'd resolved so I was upset when it got changed at the last minute. I pulled Tip aside to speak with him about it."

"What was the problem?" Thora asked. "Betty put you next to the bathroom?"

Pauline shook her head. "It was my home and that woman was giving orders in it. Everything was a power grab. When she seated herself between my husband and Clara at the head table, I lost it. Can you imagine the audacity? The woman had nerves of steel."

"Too bad she didn't have a stomach of steel," Thora said. "She might be alive today."

Bernice crossed herself again and Thora tossed a napkin at her. "Oh, stop it. That woman took the express train to hell and we all know it."

Charlie raised his brows at Kit and she smiled. "Welcome to Westdale."

"Speaking of hell, tell us about life in Hollywood," Thora said to Charlie. "Where do you buy your drugs?"

"No, tell us about when you auditioned for that cowboy movie," Phyllis urged. "I like that part of the book."

The women all began talking at once, giving Kit the chance to process what she'd learned. Pauline was a mouse of a woman who chose to speak through Tip rather than risk Betty's wrath. Betty was a powermonger who delighted in trampling over people. Aside from the location of various scars on her neighbors, Kit didn't think she'd learned anything new at all.

Chapter Six

Kit pushed open the door to Butter Beans with Charlie right behind her. The girl behind the counter broke into a nervous grin at the sight of him and nearly pushed over Sam, the barista, in a mad dash to the register.

"Mr. Owen. Double espresso?"

He smiled at the girl. "Let me guess. You read the article in *GQ* last month? Or my book?" He gave her an appraising look. "No, wait. I bet you saw me on the late night talk show."

The girl giggled as though he'd made a clever joke and turned to make the espresso.

"Wow," Sam exclaimed, running a hand through his unruly hair. "I can't believe the two of you are in the same room together. This is epic." He pulled out his phone. "Please, please with espresso on top can I take a snap and post it on Instagram?"

Charlie and Kit exchanged bemused looks.

"You don't mind, do you?" Charlie asked her. "If we do enough photo opps together, it could give your career the shot in the arm it needs to get you out of the acting dungeon." He hesitated. "If that's what you want."

"I'll do it for Sam," she said.

Ecstatic, Sam hustled out from behind the counter and stuck his head between theirs, quickly snapping a photo.

"Now just the two of you," he said.

Kit glanced over at Charlie to assess his level of acquiescence just as Sam took the picture.

"Oh Sam," Kit groaned. "I wasn't even looking."

"You were looking at me," Charlie said smoothly. "Even better."

The girl handed him his double espresso.

"Is anyone going to take my order?" Kit asked, trying not to sound impatient. She was used to being fawned over in Butter Beans. She didn't like that Charlie was usurping her spotlight.

"The lady would like an organic raspberry tea," Charlie announced.

Kit jerked her head toward him. "You remember?"

"Of course I do. We worked side by side for years." And slept side by side as well, although he thought it bad form to mention it now.

Kit felt a rush of affection for him. "I haven't had raspberry tea in a long time, actually."

"Why not?"

"I stopped doing a lot of things when I lost my job. My life." She didn't say anything more on the subject.

"You seem to be doing well enough here," he remarked, looking around. "People like you almost as much as they like me." He winked and the girl giggled again, provoking an eye roll from Kit.

"I'll get your usual, Kit," Sam offered and went back behind the counter.

"Sam is a budding screenwriter," Kit said. As much as Sam annoyed her with his parade of screenplay ideas, she felt she owed him one.

Charlie glanced at Sam. "Anything suitable for me?"

Sam's eyes nearly popped out of their sockets. "Are you kidding? Try everything I've ever written!"

Charlie grinned. "Well, let's talk a little shop, shall we?"

"I'll be over here," Kit said, accepting her drink from Sam and moving to an empty table by the window.

She flopped down in the chair with a sigh. The last time she'd sat here, she'd been with Romeo. She couldn't quite believe she and Charlie Owen were sharing coffee in Butter Beans and she hadn't wanted to scald him with it. It was surreal.

A few minutes later, Charlie plopped down in the chair beside Kit. "That guy's an amazing talent."

Kit looked at Charlie in disbelief. Sam was a nice enough guy, but she'd hardly classify him as an amazing talent. Maybe with a coffee machine...

"He's writing this screenplay about a guy who travels back in time and meets his parents when they were his age. The mom even hits on her own kid. Hilarious, right?"

Kit smacked her forehead. "Tell me you've never seen *Back to the Future*? There were three movies that pretty much covered this topic."

Charlie looked blank.

"Holy smokes, Charlie. You're a Hollywood actor. You should be a little more cineliterate."

"One semester in college and you're shaming me for my ignorance." He clucked his tongue. "What an academic snob you've become, Katherine."

"Did you give Sam your email address?" Kit asked. "I'd much rather he send you his scripts since you two seem to be on the same wavelength."

Charlie sipped from his steaming mug. "The guy's a hell of a barista, too. We could use more like him in L.A."

"No, Charlie. Actually, we couldn't." Hollywood coffee shops were overflowing with baristas hammering out screenplays during their off hours.

"What's the matter?" Charlie asked. "Are you already regretting spending unfettered time with me?"

"Actually, I'm having fun," she admitted. "Although I've been dodging Jordan's calls. He saw photos online from yesterday and went nuts."

"I like Jordan."

"Since when?" Kit demanded. They'd been mortal enemies when Kit worked with them, not unlike the Bitterbridges and Pennypackers.

Charlie grimaced. "I can't believe I'm telling you this, but I started being nice to him after you left. He's my only link to you." He slapped his thighs, clearing the sentiment from the air. "So what's on the agenda for today?"

"Have you ever been to a cricket match?" she asked.

"Cricket? No."

"Would you like to?"

"Don't those last for days?"

"If you're lucky." She raised an eyebrow.

He burst into laughter. "Why, Kit Wilder. I do believe you're flirting with me."

The pitch was a sea of foaming crests. Kit thought the crisp, white uniforms had an elegant, timeless quality.

"Isn't it cold for them out there?" Charlie asked. Spectators were few and far between today so they had a prime spot beyond the boundary.

"That's the point," Kit replied. "Most clubs play until September. These guys play all year just to prove how tough they are. It's a Westdale thing."

"Which one is your friend, Tom?" Charlie asked, scanning the matching white uniforms.

"He's the bowler." Kit pointed to the slender young man, intense and focused. In the middle of the action, he seemed to be in his element. "And Steven Pennypacker, his brother-in-law, is that one. The wicketkeeper." She gestured to the taller, broader man standing opposite Tom, behind the batsman.

"Is playing cricket really a good idea?" he queried. "Doesn't it seem a little insensitive under the circumstances?"

"He's a man who just lost his mother and possibly his bride, depending on the outcome of the investigation. For someone like Tom, cricket is an emotional outlet."

"An emotional outlet? That sounds entirely too healthy for your people," he surmised. "Surely, he should be sitting comfortably at the bar, drowning his problems in a bottle of overpriced booze."

"Tom's not like that," Kit said and covered her ears to protect them from the cold. She wished she'd worn a hat.

"So what really prompted this lengthy book tour?" she asked. "I doubt you wanted to tour every town in America."

"Change of scenery." He hesitated. "Change of relationship status."

She gave him a sympathetic smile. "Ah. Sorry."

Charlie shrugged. "Don't be. She was right to leave me," he said cryptically.

Uncharacteristically, Kit decided to leave well enough alone. She didn't like to be kicked when she was down either.

"Why Eastdale?" she asked. "Why not Philadelphia? I know geography isn't your strong suit, but it's much bigger you know."

"Ask my people. Eastdale is ugly as sin, but it's apparently full of fans." He kept his eyes on the game as he spoke, not really understanding what was happening. Watching cricket was like listening to another language that sounded vaguely like English but wasn't quite.

"How's your mom? Still in Florida?"

Charlie gave her an annoyed sidelong glance. "Please don't ask about her."

"Why? Because she asks about me?" She beamed. "I always did like her."

"She's still angry with me for cheating on you," he admitted.

As Kit turned to face him, the sound of angry yelling grabbed her attention. She jerked her head back toward the pitch, where Steven was shouting and waving a cricket bat menacingly at Tom. Kit could see the spit flying from his lips as he flipped off his helmet and rushed toward the smaller man. He pressed his chest against Tom and Tom pushed him back, unintimidated by Steven's larger size.

"I guess we know what that's about," Charlie murmured.

Kit watched in horror as Steven lifted the bat and struck Tom on the shoulder. Tom fell to the ground and all hell broke loose as the rest of the players rushed to the pitch, knocking both men to the ground and piling on.

Kit flew into action. She shrugged off her coat and sprinted headlong into the fray. The men were pushing in all directions and shouting a colorful variety of foul language. She dodged elbows and fists in an effort to reach Tom and pull him to safety. He'd suffered enough; she refused to let him add physical injuries to the growing list of unfortunate incidents.

Charlie stood in stunned silence as he watched Kit dive into the chaos without a second thought. Had she always been so fearless? He suspected the answer was yes. On the set of *Fool's Gold*, she'd been willing to do whatever stunts her insurance company allowed her to do. She'd certainly been fearless then. As for Charlie, maybe his character would have rushed willy-nilly into a manly brawl, but the actor had a handsome face to preserve.

He kept his eye trained on the pile of white uniforms, watching for a flash of Kit. He hoped she didn't sustain any injuries. He wasn't very good at playing nursemaid.

He inhaled sharply when he saw her emerge from the melee, supporting a hobbling Tom. He couldn't believe that she'd made it out of the fracas unscathed until he noticed the trail of red liquid spilling down her shirt. Not so unscathed then.

Someone from the club ran across the field with a first aid kit and Kit exchanged a few words with Tom before leaving him in the care of a professional. She returned to Charlie, still standing safely beyond the boundary. He retrieved her coat from the ground and handed it to her.

"We need to get you cleaned up," he said.

"At least it's not my blood," she said, as he took her hand and guided her away from the brawl.

In the parking lot, she passed Harley and Jamison, their car lights flashing.

"Someone called the cops?" Charlie asked. "I thought the Mayflower minions were too insular for that."

"I don't think they had a choice," she said, her expression grim. "He's sure to be arrested now, at the very least for attacking Tom. And everybody in that pileup heard Steven Pennypacker say that he wished he'd killed Betty before the wedding."

"What? Why?"

"To save his sister from marrying a coward like Tom."

Kit followed Charlie back to his hotel suite to change out of her bloody clothes. She didn't dare go back to her own house to change, not with Charlie in tow. Her neighbors would have a field day if they realized he was still in town. Thora would probably dial 'M' for murder just to get Romeo on the scene. The elderly woman had a soft spot for the detective — Kit suspected she'd go to great lengths to see them back together.

Charlie had been relieved to discover that the blood didn't belong to Kit. She'd have a nasty bruise on her hip where one of the men had kicked her, but otherwise, she was fine.

Standing in her bra and underpants, she rifled through his suitcase for something appropriate to wear.

"Don't you have anything in a small?" she called over her shoulder. "What about one of the random fans you probably slept with on your tour? Didn't you keep a memento?"

Charlie opened the connecting door, unable to hear her. "What's that?" He noticed her semi-nude body and backed away, his mouth still agape. Even without the constant training, she looked pretty good to him.

She laughed, unconcerned. She was accustomed to being in various states of undress in front of twenty-five crew members. "I hear honey works best."

He clamped his mouth closed. "Then maybe you should give it a try sometime."

"Oh, I don't know," she said coyly. "Some men like that look on me."

"I'll bet," he sneered.

Kit pulled out one of his T-shirts and held it against her chest. "It's a bit long, but it'll do the trick."

Charlie lingered for a moment before closing the door behind him. They had chemistry. Nobody disputed that. Even after they'd gotten romantically involved off-screen, they'd somehow managed to keep the energy crackling on-screen. That was unusual in their business.

Kit smiled to herself as she got dressed. She had to admit, she was enjoying herself immensely. Charlie was the perfect distraction from her problems with Romeo. Although she would never tell Charlie to his face, she missed spending time with him. Like their characters, they'd always had a lot of fun together.

In the living room, Charlie had two cups of coffee ready. He chuckled when he saw Kit sporting his T-shirt and funky golf trousers cinched with a belt.

"Who says you don't clean up nice?"

"Turns out there was blood spatter on my pants, too." She pinched the fabric of the trousers. "I didn't think you golfed."

"I don't," he replied. "They're for Mike Fusco. Remember him? One of the lighting guys. He told me to get him something pretty and the only things I could think of were golf-related."

"That was nice of you." Kit didn't remember Charlie being that involved with the crew. That had been her domain.

"After you left," he began, "I started to notice some of the things that you complained about."

"Don't notice too much," she cautioned. "Standing up for people got me fired."

Charlie handed her a steaming cup. "I don't complain for them. I'm not that brave. Since you left, though, I've made an effort to get to know some of the union guys better. They're a good bunch."

Kit settled on the sofa. "Oh good, you added milk."

"No sugar," he finished. "I remember that, too."

She stared down into her cup, unwilling to comment. Although she still harbored anger toward him, it was a little less than the day before.

"But you won't speak up for them?" she challenged.

"That's what the union is for," he replied. "I do stick my nose in now and again, though, when I think I can get away with it."

Kit wondered why Jordan hadn't told her about Charlie's new leaf. She would've liked to know that she'd made an impact on him, even a small one.

Charlie sat down beside her. "Listen, there's a New Year's Eve charity event at the art museum in Philadelphia that I was invited to."

"Don't you need to be back on the road by then?"

"I'll be in New York overnight for a signing tomorrow, but I'll come back." He placed a hand on Kit's knee. "I'd like you to spend New Year's Eve with me."

"Why? Atonement?"

Charlie patted her knee. "I could use a gorgeous actress on my arm and I hear Kit Wilder is available."

"I believe there's a scheduling conflict."

"One that you can change?" he asked, sipping his coffee. "I think there might be some people there you'd like to talk to, especially after the incident we just witnessed."

"Pennypacker people?" she queried.

He flashed a grin. "I recognized the name from the sponsorship list. You can pester their friends with inappropriate questions. Come on, the Kit Wilder I know never shrinks from a challenge. You know you want to."

Her eyes flickered to his, deciding. "Maybe."

"It'll be like old times. Consider it our last assignment. The one we should've finished together before they killed you off."

It amused her that, like her, Charlie sometimes seemed to forget that his role was fictional. She felt her resolve weaken.

"Just New Year's Eve?"

He nodded. "Then I'll be out of your gorgeous hair for good."

"All right then. I'll meet you here."

Kit sat at the long dining table in Greyabbey, enjoying a bowl of Diane's crab and corn chowder. She'd promised herself that she'd avoid her mother until after the new year, but Huntley had guilted her into attending lunch on New Year's Eve. Darn Huntley and his Southern gentility. His powers of persuasion knew no bounds, nor did his loyalty to her mother.

Huntley picked up on her bleak mood and tried to engage her in light conversation. "So are you looking forward to next semester?"

She nodded. "I am, actually. I was worried that I'd feel too out of place or too bored, but I'm neither."

"I hate to say 'I told you so,'" Heloise said, a smug smile tugging at her lips.

"Hardly. In fact, I think it's one of your favorite expressions. Definitely top ten," Kit countered, "along with 'my glass is empty' and 'would you be a dear and hand me my python.'

"And what will you be wearing tonight?" her mother asked, ignoring the jibe. Heloise knew that Kit had plans with Charlie Owen, although she refused to acknowledge it out loud. As far as Heloise was concerned, Charlie was tarred and feathered with the same brush as Romeo.

"A Halston dress that Jordan gave me," she replied. She didn't bother to say that he'd pilfered it from the set of a film that he'd worked on. Jordan was the perfect friend. He knew her size and he had access to gorgeous clothes on a regular basis.

"I do like Halston," Heloise said and returned her attention to her soup. That was the closest Kit would get to a compliment.

"I saw the pictures in the *Gazette* of you and Charlie at his book signing and afterward," Huntley said. "I suppose Crispin had advanced warning of that little reunion."

Kit shrugged innocently.

Her mother tossed a napkin onto the table in disgust. "Ugh, that wretched book. You really should sue him for defamation, not date him," Heloise snapped.

"I'm not dating him." She didn't want to tell them the real reason that she'd agreed to attend. They wouldn't approve of her involvement with the case any more than her involvement with Charlie.

"At least you're not ringing in the new year with that swarthy-looking man," her mother remarked. "He has all the charisma of a bottle of Merlot."

Kit's jaw clenched. Her mother's views on Merlot were widely known in the Greyabbey household.

Kit felt Huntley's foot press down on hers. She met his gaze; his eyes pleaded with her to remain civil.

"I would happily ring in the new year with Romeo if he were interested."

"That's just one more reason to be grateful," Heloise said airily. "I mean, if he's too intellectually stunted to tell the difference between a cheeseburger and filet mignon, why bother?"

Kit didn't love the idea of being compared to cow meat, but she was accustomed to her mother viewing her as chattel. Someone to be married off to a Breedlove or a Bitterbridge. She decided that it would be her new year's resolution to drag her mother kicking and screaming into the current century.

Kit's phone pinged and she looked down to see a text from Harley. Why would Officer Harley be texting her on New Year's Eve?

"Katherine, what have I said about technology at the table?" Heloise cast a withering glance in her direction.

"That as long as it doesn't make you look too old or too drunk, it's perfectly acceptable." She tapped on the screen and her mouth dropped open. "Holy Pilgrim. Tip Bitterbridge has been arrested for Betty's murder."

Huntley's fork clattered on the table. "I thought they arrested Steven."

"So did I." Kit stared at her screen, confused.

Heloise took the news in stride. "What's the evidence? Did they finally figure out that he was sleeping with Pauline Pennypacker?"

Kit nearly fell off her chair. "What?" Leave it to her mother to sit on a crucial piece of information.

Heloise continued to enjoy her meal. "I have no doubt they bonded over their mutual dislike of their spouses."

"Mother! Betty was your friend," Kit replied in disbelief.

Heloise flashed a look of innocence. "I didn't say that *I* disliked her. Then again, I wasn't the one married to her."

"Is that why he's been arrested?" Huntley asked. "The police discovered the affair?"

"Worse. It turns out there was an empty vial of poison," Kit said, still reading. "His housekeeper found it in the inside pocket of his tuxedo jacket." She pushed her chair back. "I need to go."

"Go where?" Heloise asked pointedly. "A phone booth to change into your super sleuth attire? Sit down, Katherine. We're having a meal."

"Tom is going to need a friend," she replied hotly. "Whether Tip's guilty or not, he's been having an affair with Tom's new mother-in-law. That's going to be tough to swallow."

"Affair or not, do you really think Tip is capable of killing his wife?" Huntley inquired.

Heloise swallowed a mouthful of her gin and tonic before responding. "Why not? I think Betty rubbed a lot of people the wrong way, including her husband."

"You rub a lot of people the wrong way, too," Kit shot back. "Should we be looking for your corpse at the next major Westdale event?"

Heloise's eyes narrowed. "Very well, Katherine. Do what you must. You always do."

"Gee, I wonder where I get it from?" Kit said, as she sailed out of the room. She didn't bother to text Harley back. She knew where to find him. Where she knew the police would be gathering evidence. Where Romeo would be gathering evidence. She jumped in her car and headed toward Oakheart.

Chapter Seven

Kit parked as far away from Romeo's black sedan as possible. She counted several vehicles in the long, circular driveway, excluding the ones that belonged to the Bitterbridges and their staff. She knew she was risking Romeo's disappointment by coming here, but she wanted to help.

The front door was wide open, sending an icy chill straight into the impressive house. She stepped into the wood-paneled foyer and glanced around to see who was there. Tom sat at the foot of the front staircase, his head in his hands.

"Tom." Swiftly, she moved forward to comfort him.

His face lifted and she could see the disbelief in his eyes. "Dora turned him in. Can you believe that? She's worked for us since I was a child."

Kit wondered whether Diane had already heard the news from her friend. "She found the vial?"

Tom nodded. "In all the confusion since the wedding, she'd forgotten to take his tuxedo jacket to the dry cleaners. He asked for it to be ready for tonight and Dora found it in his closet. She emptied the pockets as she usually does and found the vial hidden in his breast pocket. It tested positive for the mycotoxin coprine."

"So no inky cap mushrooms on the salad then," she said, more to herself. "And what does your father say about it?"

Tom looked tearful. "That he's innocent, of course. That he doesn't know how it got there. Maybe one of the Pennypackers."

"I guess they let Steven go."

Tom nodded miserably. "My shoulder's still killing me, thanks to that idiot."

"You said before that your parents didn't have the best marriage," Kit said gently. "Do you think it's possible that he used the spectacle of the wedding and the presence of the Pennypackers to make his move?" She didn't mention the affair with Pauline in case no one had told him yet. She couldn't bring herself to be the bearer of that kind of news.

Tom shook his head vehemently. "My father isn't that kind of man. If he didn't want to be married to her, he'd divorce her, not murder her."

Kit slid a supportive arm around his shoulders. She knew that emotions weren't always that simple, especially when the couple was as complex as Tip and Betty.

"Kit, what are you doing here?"

Kit recognized the large, black leather boots of Detective Romeo Moretti. Slowly, she raised her head to meet his disapproving gaze.

"I heard about Mr. Bitterbridge and wanted to see if I could do anything for Tom."

"How did you hear? You're not using a police scanner, are you?"

Across the room, she saw Harley shoot her a worried look. He didn't need to worry. She'd never rat him out.

"Diane, my housekeeper," she replied smoothly. "She's good friends with Dora."

"Of course she is."

Kit stood up to be closer to him, her heart hammering away in her chest. She felt like she hadn't seen him in forever.

"I guess you don't have plans tonight," she said, noting his casual attire of jeans and a black sweater. As usual, he looked amazing.

"Actually, I do have plans." He folded his arms across his broad chest, his jaw set.

"Oh."

"I would've thought you'd be jetting off to ski in the Alps with your former co-star."

She heard it then. The twinge of jealousy. Her spirits lifted as she said, "I don't ski."

"I thought all rich people liked to ski."

"Some rich people just like warm fires and hot chocolate." She smiled. "I can offer you both of those things back at my house, if you're interested."

Romeo shut his eyes, gathering strength. "Kit, as much as I want to be with you, the fact that you're here right now tells me that you have no intention of changing."

"Why would I?" she objected. "You already liked the girl you met. The girl who sticks her nose in Westdale business and helps you solve crimes. I hate to break it to you, but that's who I am, Romeo. You either accept it or you don't."

Romeo studied her face for a moment, as though trying to memorize her features. He didn't answer her. Instead, he simply walked away.

"Your relationship seems as doomed as mine," Tom lamented from his position on the bottom step.

Kit dropped back beside him. "They're not doomed, Tom. Just a little setback. That's all." She watched the buzz of activity in the visible rooms. "What else are they looking for?"

"Anything else that connects him to the murder."

Or to Pauline, Kit thought.

"Have you spoken to your dad since the arrest?" she asked.

"Not yet, but I called our new lawyer for a criminal defense referral. This guy's going to be thrilled to have us as a client, ruining his holidays."

Kit knew that the Bitterbridges' previous lawyer was currently sitting in a jail cell, awaiting trial for murder. Oh, the irony.

"He's a lawyer, Tom. Trust me, his holidays were already ruined."

Before heading over to Charlie's hotel, Kit drove to the Westdale Country Club to see Crispin. She wanted to touch base with him about the case and see whether he knew anything more about Tip Bitterbridge's arrest.

She checked her face in the rearview mirror and freshened her lipstick. As she hurried to escape the cold, she surveyed the assortment of luxury cars in the parking lot. The members were as privileged as ever. Kit could still picture her parents leaving for the evening in all their finery to attend New Year's Eve parties at the club. Her father's deep, rumbling laugh and her mother's brightly painted smile. Heloise stopped going to country club parties the year Kit's father died. After that, she veered toward hosting smaller, more intimate gatherings at Greyabbey. It didn't escape Kit's notice that, this year, she hadn't invited anyone at all. Huntley lived in a guest cottage on the premises. He didn't count. She felt a brief twinge of guilt for seeking her New Year's Eve fun elsewhere, but she couldn't picture herself ringing in the new year at Greyabbey. She wasn't in the mood to fend off venomous snakes or the karate stylings of marsupials.

Kit spotted her cousin pressed up against the bar, unwilling to give up his prime spot. She had to elbow her way through the crowd to reach him. She noticed several people whisper as she went by. People who either recognized her from television or as the daughter of Heloise Winthrop Wilder. In Westdale, she could never be sure.

"My favorite cousin," Crispin said and Kit heard the slight slur in his speech. "Is it midnight yet?"

She checked her diamond-encrusted watch. "Not even close."

"You didn't happen to bring Francie, did you?"

Kit smiled. She knew they were interested in each other; she wished they'd just get on with it. It wasn't like his parents would disapprove. Francie was a Musgrove. No one in Westdale would dream of rejecting a match with a Musgrove.

"She's in Aspen." The bartender approached and she leaned across the bar top to be heard over the din of the crowd. "Sparkling water with lemon, please."

Crispin gaped at her. "Kit, have you gone mad?"

"I'm not staying long."

He knocked his shoulder playfully against hers. "Admit it. You're afraid of drunk dialing your dreamboat."

She shrugged. "I'm only here to talk to you, then I'm going to the Pennypackers' event in Philadelphia. Now that Steven's been released, I may get something useful out of him. I suppose you already know the latest."

He took another sip of what Kit suspected was bourbon. "Have to print it. Hate to do it, though. Tip's such a nice man."

"A nice man who cheats on his wife?" she queried.

Crispin lifted his brows. "Wouldn't you if you were in his custom-made Italian loafers?"

"So do you think he killed her?"

Crispin pressed his lips together. "Can't imagine it, really. I mean Betty was a ball and chain and a morning star combined, but Tip's a tolerant man. And a quiet man."

"Still waters run deep?" Kit proposed.

"No, he spoke up when needed. He's not a doormat." Crispin finished his glass and set it down with a flourish.

"Then how did the vial get in his pocket?" Kit asked. She'd been mulling this over herself.

"Any Pennypacker could've put it there. They were all at the head table. They all had access. I'm going with Pauline. He was alone with her. All she had to do was slip a hand inside his jacket. Getting Betty out of the way had to be a priority for her for many reasons."

"But why would she risk framing her lover?" Kit asked. "If Pauline had feelings for Tip, why not put the vial in Mitch's jacket?"

Crispin nodded in agreement. "Your guess is as good as mine. Probably better, in fact."

"Tip left his jacket on the back of his chair. It could've been anyone who walked by." Kit's throat was beginning to strain from speaking over the noise of the crowd. "I'll do some digging tonight."

"Don't forget to have a little fun, too."

"Pace yourself, Crispin. You look like you've had enough fun already. Those red cheeks make you look like a clown."

Crispin grinned. "Good old Kit. How like your mother you are."

She punched him in the arm and he winced.

"Have you heard anything about Mitch's reaction to Tip's arrest?" she asked.

"Only that Pauline is now staying with her sister in Villanova."

"Wise woman. I wouldn't want to be around Mitch if he's angry. Or Steven for that matter."

"And yet you're putting yourself directly in their paths tonight." Crispin whistled. "No wonder Romeo worries about you."

Kit tapped her fingers on her water goblet. "About that..."

"Uh oh." Crispin examined her. "Why do I feel a favor coming on?"

Kit exhaled. "You know me too well. Remember how you told Romeo that I was interning for the *Gazette*?" He nodded and she continued. "What if I really did?"

"I would love to have you on my team," Crispin replied. "It will just be one more thing to annoy your mother, though."

She smiled. "And Happy New Year to me."

In the lobby of his hotel, a stunning figure in red caught Charlie's eye. Her hair was pulled back in an elegant chignon and she wore a body-hugging red gown with strappy heels. He hesitated, enjoying the view. They were supposed to meet at his room, but he'd gotten bored and come down for his own amusement, hoping to be recognized.

Kit headed toward the ladies room. She wanted to do a last check of hair and makeup before she went to Charlie's room. She dashed from the club so quickly that she was sure she'd smeared lipstick across her cheek or something worse. As she touched the handle to open the restroom door, a masculine hand grabbed the handle at the same time.

Kit glanced up to see Charlie, looking every bit the television hero in an Armani suit.

She smiled. "Pardon me, did you not notice the sign that reads *Ladies*?"

Charlie looked up at the door and feigned surprise.

"Would you believe there's a ridiculous line in the men's room? I don't know what they do in there, coming in groups of three and taking an eternity."

"Would you believe that I don't believe you?"

"Wouldn't be the first time now, would it?"

"Would you mind terribly if I went ahead of you?" she said sweetly.

"I suppose technically you were here first."

"And I am a lady."

"I'll take your word for it."

She narrowed her eyes at him as she swung open the door.

"I'll be right out here waiting. Don't worry about me. My bladder is tip-top."

Charlie whistled a tune and performed a little soft shoe around the corridor. A gentleman and regally dressed woman attempted to pass by and he gave them a slightly embarrassed nod before stepping aside. After a moment, Kit reappeared.

"It's all yours. Now do be a good lad and don't forget to put the seat down when you're finished."

"Now you sound like my ex-girlfriend. She was a real control freak, that one." For a heartbeat, he considered pulling her back into the restroom with him but decided against it. The last time he'd made a decision she hadn't liked, he'd ended up with a scar. All things considered, he didn't want to risk it.

Kit was familiar with two types of charity events - the stuffy kind held in Westdale and the outrageous kind held in Los Angeles where people competed to defy expectations. This evening's event fell somewhere in between.

She wasn't surprised that the Pennypackers were involved in an event that didn't include half of Westdale.

They tended to throw their hat in the ring with new money types. She hoped newly released Steven would be there. Even if he hadn't killed Betty, she still believed he had useful information. Maybe something about his mother's affair with Tip.

Flashbulbs blinded her as she and Charlie made their way down the museum's version of a red carpet and into the venue. She heard the excited murmurs of the crowd and was momentarily thrust back to her glory days.

"It's *Fool's Gold.* They're back together."

"Oh my God! It's Ellie and Jason."

Charlie squeezed her waist. "Take a breath, Wilder. It'll be okay."

It felt odd to have another man's hand on her waist. In such a short time, she'd grown accustomed to Romeo's strong arm curling around her. She felt a stab of longing and closed her eyes to regain her composure. She wasn't doing anything wrong. Romeo was not in the picture by his own volition. He even told her that he had plans. With him it had been one step forward, two steps back. The pattern of her life, in fact.

"Let's mingle," Kit said, once inside. "There must be a Pennypacker in here somewhere. I'd even take a friend of a Pennypacker."

She whipped her phone out of her bra and began tapping the screen.

"What are you doing?" Charlie asked curiously.

"Tweeting about our night. Beatrice said I should make lemonade instead of sucking lemons."

He grinned at her. "That sounds like something Beatrice would say." He glanced at the phone and his eyes widened. "You have that many followers?"

She shoved her phone back into her bra, visibly insulted. "My fans haven't abandoned me just because I'm not on the show anymore."

"Maybe you could tweet about my book," he said sheepishly.

"I think our appearance together tonight will do the trick," she retorted. Between the book signing and this charity event, tongues would be wagging throughout Hollywood. Beatrice would be pleased.

Kit spied one of the men she came to see in the far corner, chatting with another male guest. She gestured to Charlie.

"Your skills are required," she whispered. "I'd like to speak to this guy without anyone overhearing."

Charlie nodded. "Remember that episode with the jewel thief?"

"That was a multi-episode arc," she reminded him. "But I was thinking the same thing." It was nice to feel like she was on the same page with someone. On the same team. That was what she thought she had with Romeo. A true partnership. Instead, he'd shoved her back in her box under the guise of keeping her safe.

Charlie touched her gently under her chin. "Go work your magic."

Her eyes shifted and she moved gracefully across the floor to her target. She wandered comfortably through the glittering crowd, picking up a drink on her way toward the two men. She pretended they were Oscar-winning producers with a juicy role up for grabs.

With the exception of a black eye, Steven Pennypacker was all cleaned up with his Get Out of Jail Free card and appeared to be entertaining his friend with the highlights of the bloody cricket match she'd witnessed. She reached them just in time for the punchline.

"A dislocated shoulder," he said proudly.

Laughter erupted from the other man and Kit smiled appreciatively. The men noticed her immediately.

"If it isn't Tom's little savior," Steven said snidely. "Guess you couldn't save him from his parents, though."

"You didn't waste any time rejoining civilization," she said.

"I got your bling right here," the heavyset friend's voice boomed in a thick accent. He held up imaginary handcuffs. "I cannot believe this."

Despite Steven's negative vibe, she smiled and felt that pleasurable tingle of recognition. "Nice to meet you."

"Call me Sal." He stomped his feet excitedly. "Could I possibly take a photo of us? I want to show my friends on Facebook. They'll go berserk."

"Your friends *are* berserk if they'd be excited over a photo with her." Steven chugged his beer.

Kit seized her opportunity. "I'll tell you what. If I take this photo with you, would you go ask my friend Charlie Owen to take one with him?" she suggested, motioning to the part of the room where Charlie lingered. "He gets his feelings hurt when people show a preference for me." She rolled her eyes. "Actors and their egos."

"By all means," he said. "I am a big fan of his as well. Huge."

Kit linked her arm through Sal's and gave a big smile for the camera. "Hope you get a lot of likes."

"Thank you," he called over his shoulder as he made a beeline for Charlie.

Kit turned to give Steven Pennypacker her full attention. "That must've been a nasty sock in the eye."

He gave her a smug look. "Nasty business, this Bitterbridge thing."

"Yes, it is. What can you tell me about it?"

He laughed a deep, guttural laugh. "That Tip Bitterbridge is a lying sack of…"

Kit cut him off. "I'm not asking about Tip. I'm asking about you."

"Why would I be expected to know anything? I'm free. Now I'm only one of a hundred and fifty witnesses, same as you."

Kit cocked her head, studying him. Something about his demeanor rubbed her the wrong way. "All fingers point to Pennypacker involvement."

"Finger-pointing doesn't get a conviction." He tossed back the rest of his beer. "But empty vials of poison do. Now that's hard evidence."

She folded her arms across her chest, unwilling to give up on her questions yet. She couldn't quite accept that Tip was the real culprit. He was a smart man. Wouldn't he have remembered to remove the incriminating vial from his jacket pocket? He'd had ample time to dispose of it since the wedding. It was as though he truly hadn't known it was there.

"Why did you attack Tom at the cricket match and tell everyone that you wished you'd killed Betty before the wedding?" she asked.

Steven looked at her disdainfully. "There's always been bad blood between our families."

"Not between your mother and Tip, it seems."

Steven scowled and pointed his empty beer bottle at her. "Betty Bitterbridge was a bitch with a bank account. Everyone hated her but nobody stood up to her because of her money and her name. You can be damn sure that if I had actually killed her, I never would have used poison. I would've snapped her skinny neck with my bare hands." He cracked his knuckles against his beer bottle, doing his best to intimidate Kit.

Kit pushed back her shoulders and looked him in the eye. "So did you know about the affair?"

Steven's expression shifted and Kit saw the pain reflected in his hazel eyes. She could tell that he hadn't known for very long. He looked like a man still coming to grips with betrayal. Something he and Tom had in common.

"I'm no longer a person of interest," he told her. "So save your questions for someone who likes looking at you long enough to answer them."

In this moment, Kit really wished Steven Pennypacker had killed Betty. She would have loved nothing more than to see him locked up and stripped of his entitlement.

"Now that's all I have to say on the subject," he spat. "Happy Flipping New Year."

Kit fought the urge to blacken his other eye. She turned on her heel to head back to Charlie, passing Sal on the way.

"Make sure your friend doesn't drink too much," she advised. "He doesn't need any more trouble in his life right now."

Sal nodded solemnly. "You are not fooling anyone, you know."

She gave him a quizzical look.

"Charlie Owen," he said, as if that explained everything.

Kit's brow wrinkled.

Sal sighed dramatically. "Let's just say that the use of gas and electricity is completely unnecessary tonight as long as the two of you are in the room. I mean, wow. It was clear as day on the screen but to see it in real life, too." He shook his head in amazement.

Kit reddened. "Happy New Year, Sal. And may I suggest your resolution be to make better friends? Frankly, Steven Pennypacker is beneath you."

Kit threaded her way through the crowd to where Charlie was seated at a cocktail table. A glass of wine waited for her. It was just what she needed after her conversation with vile Steven Pennypacker.

"Nice to see you again, Miss. Sorry, what was your name again?" Charlie's eyes twinkled.

"Katherine Winthrop Wilder, Mayflower progeny."

"Charles Owen, actor." He reached across the table and shook her hand. This charade was for their own amusement; something they used to do on set to pass the time between takes.

"And what does your mother think of your line of work, Mr. Owen?"

"What does your mother think of yours, Miss Wilder?"

"She's happy that I am enrolled in college, but disappointed that I'm not majoring in art history."

"What are you majoring in?" he queried. "I never asked."

"No, you didn't." She paused. "Psychology."

His eyebrows lifted. "Makes sense."

Kit noticed him unconsciously swirling his wine around in his glass and smiled. "That's a lovely habit you still have."

"What is?" Charlie asked.

"The way you swirl around your wine. Very charming."

"I didn't know habits could be charming. According to my ex-girlfriend, they're all bad."

"Not this one. I've always liked this one. It makes me believe you're actually listening to me." She laughed daintily. "I can remember when you did it once with a glass of milk. Very elegant."

"We weren't always so terrible to each other, were we?" he asked softly.

"You always tormented me."

"Never. Surely, it was the other way around."

"All of America knows that you broke my heart, Mr. Owen." She still remembered how awful it had felt. She had to admit, though, his betrayal didn't hurt half as much as Romeo's absence did now.

The band began to play a slow song that Kit didn't recognize.

"How about I make it up to you?" he asked.

"How so?"

He held out his hand. "The medium of dance?"

Kit hesitated, staring at his outstretched hand.

"Don't worry, I washed it," he said.

She wore a vague smile. "It isn't that. It's just that I'm not going to get anything helpful out of Steven and I don't see Mitch. Maybe we should call it a night before one of us says something we don't mean."

"According to you, I always say things I don't mean."

She sighed. She'd been hard on him. She knew that. Not that he didn't deserve every tongue-lashing he got.

"I originally intended to humiliate you at that book signing," she admitted. Before she'd been encouraged by Thora to use Charlie's presence for other purposes.

"Bygones," he said, still smiling. "Dance with me, Ellie. Remember the end of season one?"

"The masked ball," they both said in unison. The episode was a fan favorite. When Jason and Ellie shared their first kiss. The scene was also a popular GIF.

Unable to resist the happy memory, she allowed herself to be brought onto the dance floor where other couples were already enjoying the music.

"Before I go, I want this to be my last memory," Charlie said.

"I think I'm more comfortable when we argue." She looked him in the eye.

"I think that says more about you than it does about me." Charlie cleared his throat. "So Steven's definitely not your guy, huh?"

"No," she admitted.

"Too bad. I'd love to cuff him."

"You sound like a cop," she teased.

"I do play one on TV."

She smiled. "Thank you for not including the stuff about George Clooney in your book, by the way," Kit said. "I don't love that you wrote about me, but, I admit, it could've been worse."

"I swore I'd never tell anyone that story."

She arched an eyebrow. "Except the entire cast and crew."

He began to laugh. "Kit, most of them were there. You can hardly hypnotize thirty people to forget an image like that!"

Her cheeks flamed at the memory just as a flashbulb erupted in front of them. Momentarily blinded, she gripped Charlie's arm to keep from losing her balance.

"Sorry about that," a woman said. "I wanted a candid shot before I got your attention."

The woman moved the camera away from her face and Kit's own lit up in recognition. It was Marina Lowe, one half of the husband and wife photographer team that worked the wedding. Kit didn't waste any time. She rushed to Marina, who looked slightly taken aback.

"I won't use the pictures if you don't want me to," Marina swore. "You look beautiful, though. Here, I'll show you."

Kit placed a hand on the camera, causing the woman to lower it. "I don't care about that. I want to talk to you about the Bitterbridge wedding. I remember seeing you there."

Marina nodded. "My husband took the exterior shots and I took the interior ones. No surprise that they haven't been interested in seeing their proofs. Usually, we get hounded by the clients."

Kit turned back to Charlie and held up a finger. He nodded, although she could see the disappointment etched in his handsome features. She hated to interrupt their cathartic moment, but this was important.

"Did you notice anything unusual about any of the guests?" Kit asked, pulling Marina aside. "Any strange behavior?"

Marina leaned a shoulder against the wall. "Nothing out of the ordinary. Typical wedding stuff like who's self-conscious about their body, who's nervous, who's having an affair." She shrugged. "Jacob and I handle many of the society events. That's why we're here. Jacob is outside covering the red carpet and I'm in here snapping the informal pictures."

Kit chewed her lip thoughtfully. "Did you notice any tension between the groom's parents during the photographs?"

Marina shook her head. "Not me, but my husband did. Jacob said that Betty was making comments under her breath during the ceremony and Tip told her off."

"What kind of comments?"

"Typical Betty stuff from what I understand. Pennypackers aren't good enough. There was still time for

Tom to change his mind. The same bile she'd been spewing for the last year. Tip got irate about it."

"Were you taking pictures behind the scenes before the reception started?"

"Yes, I had access to everywhere. I like to capture the spirit of the day from beginning to end. I was with Clara when she got dressed in the morning and I was in the kitchen with the catering staff taking photos of the cake."

"And your husband was...?"

"Taking pictures of the wedding party outside," Marina explained. "Between the ceremony and the reception, he took shots of the bride and groom, their families. You know how it goes."

Kit didn't know, having never been part of a wedding before, but she got the gist. "You mentioned that you could tell who was having an affair," Kit said.

Marina lowered her gaze. "I don't really talk about that stuff to anyone except Jacob. We need to respect people's privacy or we'll never work again."

"You noticed Tip and Pauline, didn't you?"

"I wasn't one hundred percent sure," she admitted, "but the signs were there."

"So were they the nervous ones?" Kit asked. "Afraid of getting caught maybe?"

Marina shook her head. "Not them. I usually see jitters in the bride or the groom, but it wasn't them either." Her smile faded. "It was the mother of the groom this time. I think she couldn't believe that her son was actually going through with the wedding. It seemed to unnerve her."

Kit swallowed hard. "You think Betty Bitterbridge was nervous?" Kit wondered how on earth Marina could tell that Betty Bitterbridge was nervous about anything. The woman was five and a half feet of pure steel. "What makes you think so?"

"She'd been barking orders at the staff about everything under the sun. When to serve out the champagne and appetizers and which plates went to which members of the wedding party. Once she'd scared the staff away, she pulled a small vial from her…" Marina indicated her cleavage. "Anyway, I've seen enough women who self-medicate."

Kit's heart stopped. "Did you see what she did with it?"

"I didn't hang around long enough to see. She glared at me and I hightailed it out of there."

Kit's brain was in overdrive. "You told me before that someone had expressly forbidden video at the wedding. Who forbade it? The bride and groom?"

"No." Marina's voice dropped to a whisper. "It was Betty Bitterbridge."

Kit didn't wait to ring in the new year. She couldn't celebrate knowing that an innocent man was sitting in jail. That a son was sitting in an empty house, believing that his father had murdered his mother at his wedding.

She grabbed Charlie by the wrist and dragged him out of the venue.

"Where are we going?" he asked.

"You said we make a great team." She gave him a meaningful look.

"Where are we going?" he asked. "To the police station?"

"Nope. Somewhere closer." She flashed him a mischievous look. "Buckle up, Charlie. We're crashing a party in South Philly."

Romeo had told her that he had plans. At first, Kit thought maybe he had a date, but she quickly wised up. She knew how close he was to his family. No way was he spending New Year's Eve with a room full of strangers in a bar or club.

"Are you sure about this?" Charlie asked, as she parallel parked on a busy urban street. Although she hadn't had the pleasure of meeting Romeo's family yet, she paid attention to all of his stories. She knew where his mother and father lived. She also knew that their house was the center of the Moretti universe. It didn't take a detective to work out his location tonight.

"Couldn't you call him?" Charlie asked, stopping on the sidewalk. "Tell him to meet you outside. I'll wait in the car."

Kit couldn't believe her ears. "Charlie Owen, are you afraid to meet him?"

He slumped his shoulders. "You said he's tall."

"And broad-shouldered." She sighed. "And muscular."

He narrowed his eyes. "Okay, I get the picture."

Kit laughed. "Charlie, you're an incredibly handsome man and you know it. America knows it. Now be my teammate one last time and step up."

She held out her hand and he took it.

"If I get a black eye, I'm sending you the bill," he grumbled, as Kit knocked loudly on the front door. The music inside was blaring and Kit wondered whether anyone would even hear them.

The door flew open and a small, dark-haired woman squinted at them. "Are you lost?"

"We're looking for Romeo," Kit said. "Is he here?"

The woman looked her up and down. "It's New Year's Eve."

"I know and I'm sorry," Kit said, "but this is important."

"One of his cases, right?" the woman asked, her irritation evident. "It's always work with that boy." She pulled open the door and ushered them inside. "Everyone's in the kitchen playing Dama."

Romeo nearly dropped the beer bottle in his hand when he saw Kit step through the doorway of his parent's kitchen with the actor in tow. What in the hell was she doing bringing that filth to his doorstep? He stared at her, momentarily distracted by her red dress. If she wanted him jealous...Well, he was jealous.

"Romeo, can we talk to you?" Kit asked. She seemed anxious.

He pushed his chair back. "Everyone, this is Kit and..."

"Charlie," he said.

"Kit and Charlie, this is my family."

The woman who opened the door gasped. "You're Kit? You look so much prettier in person."

The room full of Morettis and DeLucas turned to gape at her.

"Kit, sit down," an older woman said, shoving Kit toward the table. "What can I get you to drink?"

"It's not a social call, Nonny," Romeo scolded her.

"This is Nonny?" Kit asked. She smiled at the white-haired woman. "I've heard so much about you."

The woman smiled, showing off her dentures. "Why not a social call? It's New Year's Eve."

"I have something to tell Romeo about a case he's working on," Kit explained.

"She does that a lot," Romeo added.

"Charlie, you sit," the older woman insisted. "Do you like tiramisu?"

"I do, actually."

She squeezed his arm. "Ooh. Very strong, this one." She waved at Romeo and Kit. "You go talk. We take care of Charlie."

Romeo glared at Kit as he ushered her upstairs to an empty bedroom. It was a small room, littered with trophies and posters.

"I'm amazed that you would come here and flaunt that idiot in my face." His ears were bright red, a sure sign that he was not too happy with Kit.

"I'm sorry, but we were at this charity event together. I couldn't very well leave him there."

"He's a big boy. He knows how to call a cab."

Kit sighed. "I'm not here to fight with you, Romeo. I'm here to help. Tip didn't kill his wife. You've got the wrong guy." Again.

Romeo pressed his fingers to his temples. "The vial was found hidden in his pocket."

"But I don't think he put it there." She told him what Marina had seen.

Romeo paced the floor in front of her, his hands thrust angrily into his pockets.

"She sees the victim with something suspicious in a vial, the victim later dies, and she doesn't think it's worth telling the police?"

Kit could see the tendon tightening in his neck.

"You don't understand, Romeo. She works all the high society parties and weddings. It's perfectly normal to see a woman like Betty Bitterbridge self-medicating, especially during a wedding."

"Except she wasn't self-medicating. That stuff was poison."

Kit pressed her lips together. "I know that, but what Marina saw didn't seem out of the ordinary to her. Betty was the uptight mother of the groom. In Marina's mind, she was trying to relax." Kit shrugged. "I wouldn't bat an eye if I saw my mother whip out a vial and she and Betty are pretty similar." She paused. "Were similar."

Romeo dragged a hand through his thick, dark hair. "You people are crazy, you know that?"

Kit's stomach clenched. "Hey, please don't lump us all together. I don't consider gin the breakfast of champions and I don't pop pills unless they're Flintstone vitamins. I can't resist those."

Romeo glanced at Kit, realizing the harshness of his words. His expression calmed. "I'm sorry, Kit. I didn't mean that. It's just frustrating. She should have come forward. I mean, Betty's husband is sitting in custody."

"Maybe that's what Betty wanted," Kit suggested. "Maybe that's why she put it there. She was a vindictive woman."

"You're sure Marina isn't lying?"

Kit gave a vehement shake of her head. "She has no reason to lie. She didn't even remember what she'd seen until we spoke," Kit assured him. "The moment was that uneventful in her mind."

"You know what this means, don't you?" he asked and Kit nodded. She knew exactly what this meant.

Betty Bitterbridge wasn't murdered after all. It was suicide.

Chapter Eight

Kit slept in her own bed that night, despite Charlie's best efforts to lure her back into his. As charming and handsome as he was, Kit wasn't tempted. Her heart belonged to Romeo, whether he wanted it or not. She'd felt his eyes burning a hole in her back as she and Charlie left the row house and had fought the urge to turn back and launch herself into his arms.

Despite her fatigue, she barely slept, tossing and turning with thoughts of the Bitterbridges and Pennypackers. She was already wide awake the next morning, reading a Katharine Hepburn biography, when Charlie rang her bell to say goodbye.

"Happy New Year," he said, looking like a million bucks. He glanced down at Kit's feet and smiled. "Still wearing those sexy slippers, huh?"

Kit laughed. "They're still my longest relationship."

"You know my feelings about threesomes," he said, his eyes twinkling.

She wiggled each bunny. "By all means, buy yourself a pair. How'd you sleep?"

"Alone," he replied grimly. "You're the worst New Year's date ever."

"I never said it was a date."

"I don't think your detective friend liked me very much," Charlie said. "He kept scowling at me."

"That's because Romeo never watched our show. Your show," she corrected herself.

"And because you told him what a scumbag I am," he guessed.

Kit pretended to look thoughtful. "I may have said a few things that painted you in an unfavorable light."

"Shocker." His grin broadened. "I'm glad I came. This was more fun than I've had in ages. I can always count on you for a good time."

"After everything that's happened," Kit said, "it's nice to know we still work well together."

Charlie's features softened and he stroked his thumb over her cheek. "I am sorry about everything, Kit. Truly. Do you forgive me?"

Kit nodded. "I do."

"Maybe we'll get to work on another project together someday," he said. "If they ever lift the ban on you, that is."

"Maybe." She was noncommittal. The truth was, the more time she spent in Westdale, the less she missed Hollywood. She was building a new life and, to her surprise, she didn't hate it.

Charlie brushed his lips against hers. "Take care of yourself, Kit."

"Safe travels."

He got into his rental car and she watched her past drive away. Once he disappeared around the corner, Kit's thoughts turned to college and her new friends, and to a certain handsome detective. To what she hoped was her future.

Chief Riley stood in the banquet room of the Westdale Country Club, wiping away the relentless beads of sweat on his brow. He didn't want to be here on official business. Didn't like to be the bearer of this type of news. He had an obligation to his people, though, and the Bitterbridges and Pennypackers were most definitely his people. He figured the club was neutral territory as well as the easiest place to gather this particular group together on New Year's Day.

"Rich, I hope you come with news of more rock solid evidence against Tip." Mitch glanced up from his Bloody Mary, bleary-eyed and miserable.

"I'll wait for Tom and Steven, if you don't mind. I'd rather only have this conversation once."

"Suit yourself."

They didn't wait long. Steven sauntered in from the bar area with a beer in his hand. "Hair of the dog," he said, taking a swig.

Tom practically took the door off its hinges on his way in, eager to hear the chief's news. The chief's expression soured when he saw that Kit was hot on his heels.

"This is a private matter," the chief told her.

"I think you'll find it's quite a public one," Kit replied. "And I'm covering it for the *Westdale Gazette*."

Chief Riley rolled his eyes in annoyance. "In that case, I'll need to have a word with Crispin."

"Have several words," Kit said. "By all means, string a whole sentence together. Doesn't change the fact that I'm going to stay here and listen to your update on the case."

"I knew I should've had this in my office," the chief grumbled.

"Where's Clara?" Tom asked, looking around the room. "I thought she'd be here."

"She didn't want to come," Steven replied.

"She spent New Year's Eve with her mother in Villanova," Mitch said bitterly.

"I guess she didn't want to end up a corpse for the new year," Tom muttered.

"Maybe you haven't noticed," Mitch said, draining his Bloody Mary, "but I'm not the one under arrest."

"I don't understand why you're letting her stay," Steven complained, glaring at Kit. "It's bad enough that she crashed an invitation only party last night."

"My date was invited," she pointed out.

Tom moved to stand beside Kit. "I'd like her to stay. She's been incredibly supportive of Clara and me. Unlike some people."

"And a lot of good that did," Mitch snapped. "You're not exactly together, are you?"

Tom shot him an angry look. "Let's hear what the chief has to say."

"The good news is that, as soon as we can drag someone into the office on a holiday, your father will be released," Chief Riley told Tom.

Tom closed his eyes and exhaled.

"Released on what grounds?" Mitch demanded. "I hope this means you've identified the real killer."

Chief Riley studied the floral carpet. "We have."

Steven glanced around at the gathered group. "Is it one of us?"

"No," the chief replied firmly and Kit heard the collective sigh of relief. "Based on new evidence, we now believe that Betty's death was a suicide."

Tom balked. "What?"

The chief swiped a cloth napkin from a nearby table and wiped his perspiring forehead. "I'm sorry, Tom. I know this must be difficult to hear."

"Because it isn't true," Tom insisted. "My mother was a manipulative woman but to kill herself?" He shook his head adamantly. "She would never do such a thing."

"What about the empty vial that was found in Tip's pocket?" Steven asked.

"We believe that Betty put it there herself after she'd emptied the contents into her own plate of caviar."

Kit understood the delicacy of the matter. On the one hand, the chief needed to explain why they'd decided on suicide. To do so, however, meant discussing the deceased in a somewhat unfavorable light. To her grieving son, no less.

"Think about it, Tom," Chief Riley said. His voice was so soft, Kit barely recognized it. "Everyone in Westdale knew how unhappy she was about the marriage. She didn't bother to hide it. Every suspect we had suffered through unpleasant conversations with your mother. Your mother had true grit and she was determined to derail the marriage at any cost."

Tom's shoulders drooped and he removed his sweater. The temperature in the room seemed to have increased tenfold since Chief Riley dropped his bombshell.

"It would be the perfect revenge," Steven pointed

out. "Cast a cloud over the day and drive a permanent wedge between you and Clara. Seems to have worked, too."

Under the circumstances, Kit wondered why Betty bothered to hide her antipathy during the reception. Why give such an upbeat speech if she planned to ruin the day? Maybe to make her death that much more poignant. Or because she never expected her death to be ruled a suicide. After all, if she'd known about Tip's affair with Pauline, she wouldn't put it past Betty to take swift, vengeful action.

Tom seemed to share her thinking. "Do you think she meant to frame my father?"

Chief Riley patted his shoulder sympathetically. "Hard to say. It's certainly possible."

"Mother was vindictive," Tom agreed. "I guess she decided that she didn't want to live in a world where Bitterbridges found happiness with Pennypackers."

"It's not like we were thrilled with the idea at first," Mitch said. Kit noted a flatness in his tone. She got the sense that Mitch Pennypacker was experiencing an unfamiliar emotion — sympathy for the Bitterbridges.

Tom dug the toe of his shoe into the carpet. "I feel like it's all my fault. How can Clara and I make a fresh start knowing that Mother was willing to sacrifice her own life to keep us apart?"

Mitch walked over to his son-in-law and clapped him on the shoulder. "You're a grown man now, Thomas. Time to step out from behind your mother's domineering shadow and act like one."

"I'd like to see my father," Tom said to the chief.

"Don't worry, Tom. We'll make that happen today."

Tom nodded and shook the chief's hand. "Thank

you, sir. I appreciate your hard work on this case. I know it hasn't been easy."

Chief Riley's eyes flickered momentarily to Kit's. She caught a hint of guilt in his expression, an acknowledgement that maybe Kit had played a role in the outcome.

"I'll walk out with you," Kit told Tom.

They made their way through the empty club and out the front door.

"You didn't seem surprised," Tom said, as a blast of cold air hit them.

"I *may* have spoken to a witness who saw your mother with the telltale vial," Kit admitted. And here she thought her own mother was the worst kind of martyr. Betty had her beat by a country estate mile. "I passed along the information to the police." She hesitated. "I thought it best to let them handle the rest."

"At least my father is a free man," he said, more sullen than Kit would have liked.

"Do you think you and Clara can work through this?" Kit asked. "Start off the new year together, as a married couple?"

"I don't want Mother's death to be in vain. If I stay married to Clara, then I'm basically telling the world that I don't care that my mother killed herself because of my actions." He shook his head. "That's not what a Bitterbridge would do. Family comes first."

"But isn't Clara your family now?" Kit suggested gently.

She felt awful for Tom. Either way, he lost. And so did Clara.

Chapter Nine

Kit was in the middle of a weird dream that involved Romeo, trophies in his childhood bedroom, and a tray of baked ziti when the sounds of reality began to buzz around her.

"Kit, you need to see this!"

"Open up, lazybones or I'll use my pistol on this cheap doorknob!"

Kit heard the insistent voices, urging her awake. She sat up and blinked. Ugh, she'd fallen asleep in front of the television again. She wiped the drool from her cheek and dragged her body to the front door.

"New Year's Eve has come and gone, ladies," she said. "Feel free to resume your regularly scheduled bedtimes."

Phyllis nudged Thora, who stood beside her on the front step. "It's this one's fault. She finally found my secret stash of absinthe."

"Absinthe?" Kit queried.

"She had a companion from Prague," Thora explained.

"A long time ago," Phyllis said with a deep sigh. "Evsen. He was very sweet and...flexible."

Kit winced at the thought and stepped aside to let them in. "What brings you here if you have potent contraband at your house?"

Phyllis held up her phone.

"Phyllis, you know perfectly well how to use your phone. Save the incompetent old woman act for the men at Best Buy." Kit turned to head back to the sofa.

"Wake up that brain of yours," Thora said. "Look at what's on the phone."

Kit yawned and took the phone. "YouTube?" She eyed them both.

"What? We like cat videos as much as the next old woman," Phyllis said defensively.

Thora laughed and elbowed Phyllis. "Remember that one with the cat attacking the laptop?" She snorted. "The guy's coffee scalded the hell out of his crotch."

"Sounds hilarious," Kit said flatly. She tapped the screen and her brow furrowed. "Hey, this is from the wedding."

"Smarter than she looks," Thora said to Phyllis, who nodded triumphantly.

Kit watched as Betty delivered her speech. She remembered it well, given the circumstances. She listened to Betty again as she spoke about the greatness that she expected from her son. How he was the future of the Bitterbridge line and she'd be there to support him every step of the way. She certainly didn't sound like a woman about to commit suicide in front of her family and friends.

Given the low quality, she guessed that someone had filmed it on a phone.

Kit continued to watch in horror as Betty drained her champagne after Tom's toast and then dropped like a stone, her body jerking dramatically as she fell across the table. That was some heart attack. It was just as upsetting to witness the second time around. The video stopped at the moment Romeo rushed to the table.

"Who uploaded this?" Kit asked, outraged.

The elderly women shrugged. "Someone who goes by Gamer321."

Kit checked to see whether Gamer321 had uploaded any other videos. There were no others from the wedding, but plenty that involved Minecraft, World of Warcraft and the Kim Kardashian app. Unfortunately, Gamer321 didn't appear or speak in any of the videos.

"Do you think it could be the murderer?" Phyllis asked.

"The video is like his serial killer trophy," Thora added.

"Betty killed herself," Kit said. "Besides, serial killers don't usually share their trophies. They're personal items, kept as mementos."

Thora glanced at her suspiciously. "Sounds like you know an awful lot about it."

"Season three of *Fool's Gold*," Kit said. "We had an eight episode serial killer arc. He kept locks of his victim's hair and made himself a wig."

Thora waved a dismissive hand. "In my day, men kept locks of hair as a declaration of love and admiration for a woman." She fluttered her eyelashes regretfully. "How times have changed."

"So is it too late to call Romeo?" Phyllis asked. "He'll want to see this."

Kit bit her lip. She didn't want to push her luck with him. Showing up at his parent's house was bad enough.

"I don't know..."

Thora whipped out her phone. "His number is right here." She thrust the phone into Kit's other hand.

"Why do you need me?" she asked. "You could have called him yourself and told him what you found."

Thora and Phyllis exchanged guilty glances.

"You two need to stop meddling!" she insisted. "Romeo has made it clear that he does not like me to interfere with police business and I don't like you to interfere with my love life."

"What love life?" Thora shot back. "You're falling asleep on your couch in fuzzy pajamas. With your youth and that body, Romeo should arrest you for neglect."

Kit shut her eyes. "Don't be ridiculous."

"This isn't meddling, Kit," Phyllis assured her. "This is being a Good Samaritan."

Kit stared at the phone in her hand. She really did want to hear his voice. Then again, she didn't want to hear it yelling or telling her why he couldn't see her.

"How about I call Harley or Jamison?" she asked. "They can tell Romeo."

Thora snatched back her phone. "Yellow belly," she hissed.

Kit handed back the other phone to Phyllis. "I'm sorry to disappoint you."

"No absinthe for you!" Phyllis said.

"That's probably for the best," Kit told them. "I tried it once. It ended with a llama in my kitchen and a drunken phone call to George Clooney." At the mention of George, Kit snapped her fingers. "Forget the police. I know who uploaded this video."

Once Kit changed out of her pajamas and ran a brush through her hair, it didn't take long to track down Gamer321. Accompanied by Phyllis and Thora, she ended up at a large house on Penn Road right near the country club.

"I thought so," Thora said. "The Wallingfords live here. I knew Horace Wallingford once upon a time."

"In the carnal sense," Phyllis added, unhelpfully.

Kit threw her hands over her ears. "TMI, ladies."

They rang the bell twice and waited a good five minutes before a disheveled teenaged boy pulled open the front door. Leonard Wallingford stared at the trio, his glasses slipping down his nose.

"Wow," he breathed, his eyes alighting on Kit.

Kit leaned against the doorjamb, her coat hanging open. "Hi, there. We're looking for Gamer321." Her voice was like honey.

Leonard opened his mouth but no words came out.

"You've paralyzed him," Thora complained. "Put your boobs away before you do permanent damage."

Kit straightened and buttoned the top of her coat. "You see, I subscribe to his YouTube channel and I've been dying to meet him."

Leonard smiled and Kit spotted his Invisalign braces. "I'm Gamer321."

"Thought so." She brushed past him and Thora and Phyllis trampled his toes behind her. "Take us to your computer, Leonard."

His eyes popped. "Wait, you know my name?"

"Of course I do. You're a Wallingford in Westdale." She clapped her hands. "Computer. Now."

"Uh, okay. No problem." She could see Leonard's Adam's apple moving up and down. He hurried ahead of them to a staircase and gestured for them to follow him to the lower level.

"He has a lair," Phyllis whispered loudly. "Be careful, it could be evil."

As it turned out, the entire lower level of the house was Leonard's lair. It was easily two thousand square feet of teenage glory. One quarter of the space was devoted to electronics and that was where Leonard went to sit at an oversized black desk.

"I'm a huge fan," the teenager said. Ellie Gold was in his bedroom, flanked by two elderly bodyguards. The guys would never believe him. "I was so stoked when I found out you were going to be at the wedding. You're the only reason I went. I usually stay home and play computer games."

"No kidding," Thora remarked.

"Always nice to meet a fan. Now scoot." Kit bumped him off the chair so that she could sit down. "What's your password, Leonard?"

When he didn't respond, she glanced up at him. He shifted awkwardly and mumbled something unintelligible.

"Leonard," she snapped.

"It's BlingRightHere."

Kit paused, her fingers hovering over the keyboard. "Seriously?"

He nodded profusely, wiping his nose on his sleeve.

"Oh," Phyllis said. "He's *that* kind of fan."

She typed in the password and the other women moved closer, pointing to the wedding folder on the screen.

"Does that say *wedding*?" Thora asked, peering closer.

"Yes." Kit double-clicked and counted ten short videos.

"You're sure these are the only ones?" she asked.

"Yes," Leonard said. "My phone ran out of juice after the police came or I would've recorded them, too."

"What a budding photojournalist you are," she said, clicking open the first video. "Crispin might have a spot for you down the road."

Her own face smiled back at her. She was chatting with Francie and Charlotte before the arrival of the bride and groom.

"I really liked your dress," Leonard said, in a way that made Kit's skin crawl. She rolled the wheels of the chair back over his toe. He yelped and backed away.

"No commentary," she ordered.

"You might not want to watch all of the videos," Leonard said.

"Why?" Thora demanded. "Is there porn?"

"No," Leonard stammered. "Not from the wedding, anyway."

Kit quickly understood why Leonard tried to dissuade her from watching all of the videos. The footage seemed to focus more on their body parts than anything else. A close-up of Charlotte's chest. A shot of Francie's calves. Kit's backside.

"Usually, I can tell if a guy is a breast man," Kit said, "but, Leonard, you're all over the map."

"These are disgusting and juvenile," Phyllis said. "I hope you don't intend to upload any of these."

"And Kit's ass looks like it's made of Jell-O," Thora added. "You can't show that to the American public. She'll never work again."

"I don't know," Phyllis began, "there seems to be a market for that sort of look."

Leonard shook his head adamantly. "I wasn't going to. I only uploaded the one with Mrs. Bitterbridge because it was so cool."

Three heads whipped around to glare at him.

"Not cool, but..." He squirmed, fiddling with the Star Wars figures on his bookcase. "It's not every day you capture somebody's death on video."

"You're right, Leonard," Kit said. "It's not cool. Not cool at all."

Kit continued clicking through the videos, looking for clues.

"The only other one I almost uploaded was the one of Charlotte because people like physical comedy," he told them. "Stuff like that gets lots of likes."

Kit's radar pinged. "Which one of Charlotte?"

"When she nearly takes out the entire head table," Leonard said and started to laugh at the memory. One icy look from Kit shut him up. "How drunk was she anyway?"

"She wasn't drunk," Kit insisted. "That's just how

she is." Kit wasn't in the mood to explain Charlotte's dyspraxia to Leonard. She had more pressing matters.

She opened the video in question and watched Francie and Charlotte whisper to one another, clearly discussing Crispin who was visible in the background.

"I don't remember this," Kit said.

"You'd gone to talk to your mother," Leonard said. "I didn't want to risk filming *her*."

"Don't worry. Her image doesn't show up on film anyway," Kit said wryly.

She watched as Francie and Charlotte tried to look nonchalant, planning to casually bump into Crispin. In typical Charlotte fashion, her right foot got hooked on the bride's chair and she tripped, nearly taking the tablecloth with her.

"This is so embarrassing," Phyllis said. "Do we need to see this?"

"Keep watching. She plays it off like a boss," Leonard assured them.

"Years of experience," Kit said.

They continued to watch as Charlotte quickly recovered, straightening and looking around to see if anyone had noticed. As her gaze swept over the room, she caught sight of something on the head table in front of her and broke into a huge smile. She tugged on Francie's dress.

"What is she doing?" Thora asked, squinting. "Why is she playing with the serving platter?"

"That caviar was sick," Leonard enthused. "My mom caught me trying to snake her portion and nearly bit my hand off."

"Sick means it was good," Thora explained to Kit,

as if she didn't already know.

Kit's mouth dropped open. "Oh, no."

"I know," Phyllis said. "You can see Francie's bra strap. You should tell her to wear a strapless bra next time."

"Not that," she said, turning to look at them. "I know what really happened to Betty."

In the back booth at Provincetown Pancakes, Romeo watched the video a second time.

"And you spoke with Charlotte already?" he asked.

Kit nodded. "She explained what she was doing, but I figured it was something like that."

"Do you mind if I call to confirm her story?"

"I'd be surprised if you didn't." She tapped her fingers on the table. "Are you angry that I'm the one who showed you the videos?"

"No," he said softly. "But you could've just told me about them over the phone. Or sent me a link. Just because I never watched your show doesn't mean I don't know how to use YouTube."

Kit slunk back in her seat. "I know."

She felt his hand reach across the table and cover her own. "So I can only assume that you asked me to meet you here because you miss me."

Kit glanced up from her lap and met his dark gaze. "Of course I miss you. What do you think?"

He shrugged. "I think maybe you got back together with your TV star boyfriend."

Kit's mouth dropped open. "You think what?"

"You showed up with him at my parents' house.

Maybe you wanted to make a point." Romeo pulled up a different video on his phone. "Plus, you're not the only one with access to YouTube." He handed her the phone. It was a video of Kit and Charlie walking the red carpet on New Year's Eve. Their arms were linked and they were laughing.

"We're actors, Romeo," she explained. "It was for the cameras. We're not together, I swear. In fact, he's been gone for ages." Okay, maybe *ages* was a stretch.

"So have I," he said quietly.

"I've noticed."

He squeezed her fingers in his strong hand. "I read the rest of his book. He ends up saying some pretty nice things about you." He paused. "And some pretty crappy things about himself."

Kit nodded. "I didn't want to read it, but I was glad I did."

"I thought maybe you'd want to go back to him, knowing that he regretted the way things ended between you. How he treated you."

"Is that why you're still avoiding me?" Kit asked, incredulous. "Not because of the case?"

Romeo shook his head and swiftly moved to her side of the table. "You were right. I shouldn't try to change you." He raked a hand through his thick hair. "Hell, I don't really want you to change. I like spirited and resourceful Kit Wilder. By the time I got my head on straight, you and Mr. Celebrity were joined at the hip and I worried that I was too late. That I'd lost you to someone else."

Kit took his rugged face in her hands and kissed him.

"You haven't lost me," she promised. "I'm right

here."

Chapter Ten

Two hours later, Kit and Romeo drove up the winding path to the Pennypacker estate. Judging from the line of luxury cars, her message had been received.

They barely knocked on the front door before being ushered into the marble-infested living area.

"What's the meaning of this?" Tip Bitterbridge demanded. "Why have you told us to meet you here of all places?"

Kit noticed Clara and Tom eyeing each other longingly from across the room. She hoped this next bit of news would bring them closer together — permanently.

"If you could all relax and have a seat, we'll explain everything," Kit assured him.

Everyone was there, as requested. The Bitterbridges, Tom and Tip. The Pennypackers, Mitch, Steven, Clara and even Pauline. Kit noticed that Mitch and Pauline sat close together and wondered whether they'd decided to work things out. That would explain Tip's irritated tone.

"We hope to end this feud between your families once and for all," Kit said.

Mitch and Tip eyed each other warily.

Romeo directed his remarks at the Bitterbridge side of the room. "You should know that Elizabeth Bitterbridge did not commit suicide."

A gasp rippled through the room.

"But Chief Riley..." Tip began.

Romeo held up a hand and nodded, understanding his confusion. "It did appear to be suicide, but new evidence has come to light." He glanced at Kit. "Thanks to the intrepid efforts of this young woman."

Kit blushed. Not only was Romeo not chastising her for getting involved, he was complimenting her. It didn't get much better than this.

Tip cast a suspicious eye across the room. "So we're back to murder, are we?"

"Don't look over here," Mitch growled. "A Pennypacker would never stoop to using a cheap poison like coprine. For Pete's sake, inky caps can be found in any common forest. We'd splash out on something unique like heavy water."

Romeo moved between the parties, noticing that Tip's hands were now balled into fists.

"It's not exactly murder," Romeo said and Tip's arms dropped to his side.

"What does that mean? Not exactly murder?" he queried.

Tom blinked. "If it's not murder and it's not suicide, then what's left?"

"An accident," Kit said. "Although it seems that there was likely an attempted murder."

"It can hardly be considered attempted when the victim actually dies," Tip countered.

"But the victim didn't die," Kit explained. "Not the intended victim, anyway." She turned to face Clara, who sat perfectly still on the lipstick red settee. "There was a reason that Betty had insisted on Beluga caviar and not salmon roe."

"Filthy greed?" Steven suggested.

"Color. Salmon roe wasn't dark enough to disguise the poison. Beluga, on the other hand, was the right color and had the strong flavor necessary to mask the taste."

"But why would she need to disguise the flavor if she was the one eating it?" Clara asked.

Kit glanced at Romeo and he nodded for her to continue. "Because the portion of caviar laced with poison wasn't intended for her. It was intended for you." Kit gave Clara a sympathetic look. "It's doubtful you would've noticed it or tasted it thanks to the strong flavor of the caviar. And that was her plan."

Clara gripped the edge of the settee. "I ate the caviar when I came to the table. It was the first thing I did. I was so hungry after starving myself all day."

"That's what she was counting on," Romeo told her.

"It explains why her speech was so uncharacteristically happy," Kit continued. "She figured that in a few, short minutes, she'd be rid of you or, at the very least, she would have ruined your special day."

Clara's hand flew to her chest. "That's why she was so adamant about the menu and the seating arrangements."

"So what happened?" Mitch asked. "How was she foolish enough to ingest it herself?"

"One of the wedding guests stopped to admire the vintage serving platter that was used on the head table. Apparently, it reminded her of a family heirloom." Kit didn't think it was necessary to name and shame Charlotte. "The plates rotate, you see, like a Lazy Susan. She turned it to show a friend and didn't bother to spin it back to its original position." She shrugged. "It's not like she knew one of the dishes was laced with poison."

"So Betty ate the caviar that she'd intended for Clara," Tip said softly.

Tom's gaze shifted to Clara and Kit could see the relief wash over him.

"I'm sorry, Mr. Bitterbridge," Kit said. "In some ways, it was better to think that she'd killed herself, but that wouldn't be right."

Tip's head drooped forward. "No, of course not."

"What if she'd been successful?" Steven asked. "What if Clara had died? Wouldn't Betty have been the prime suspect?"

"We have a couple of theories," Kit said. "For starters, she was a woman on a mission who was at the end of her rope. All her scheming prior to the wedding had failed to produce the desired result."

"She also had friends in very high places," Romeo added. "She might have banked on her friendship with Chief Riley and other powerful people to save her hide."

"Wouldn't be the first time," Kit muttered under her breath.

"But she put the vial in your jacket, Dad," Tom remarked, his brow creased. "Do you think she meant to frame you?" He didn't say *because of the affair*, but everyone knew that was what he meant.

Tip blotted his glistening forehead with a spotted handkerchief. The whole conversation made him deeply uncomfortable. "I'd like to think that it was for convenience only. That she'd intended to remove it later and dispose of it."

"It's possible that she didn't intend to kill Clara," Romeo said. "Coprine isn't generally fatal. It's possible that Mrs. Bitterbridge only intended to humiliate Clara by making her violently ill at the wedding."

"Alcohol mixed with coprine is a dangerous combination," Kit clarified. "Mrs. Bitterbridge knew that Clara would be drinking more than usual in the days leading up to the wedding as well as at the reception."

"But Mother drank five times the amount that Clara did," Tom murmured.

Nothing new there, Kit thought to herself.

"She was also drunk at the rehearsal dinner the night before," Tip admitted. "I had to put her to bed."

"In her case, the poison mixed with copious amounts of alcohol triggered a heart attack," Romeo explained.

"So we'll never really know what her intentions were," Clara said softly.

"I can't believe she tried to hurt you," Tom said, gazing at his beloved. "If she weren't already dead, I'd kill her myself."

"Oh, Tom," Clara cried.

He couldn't keep his distance a moment longer. He practically leapt across the room, meeting Clara halfway. He swept her into his arms and they clung to each other, murmuring apologies and promises.

"We appreciate you bringing us the truth," Mitch said, one eye trained on the reunited couple. "Lord knows I wasn't in favor of the marriage, but seeing how in love they are, how could I not come around?"

Kit watched in amazement as Mitchell Pennypacker extended his hand to Tip Bitterbridge.

"I'd like to propose a truce," Mitch said. "Everything that happened up until now is water under the Lenapehoking Bridge. And I do mean everything." They shook hands and Tip smiled at Clara.

"Welcome to the family," he said.

Kit stood on the front stoop of the modest row house, waiting for Romeo to park the car. It was close to freezing so he'd dropped her off like a gentleman and circled the block for a spot. Although the wind was bitterly cold, she refused to knock until Romeo was beside her. This was his family, after all.

"Ready?" he asked, bounding up the steps. He snaked a hand around her waist and squeezed.

"As I'll ever be. They probably hate me for showing up here on New Year's Eve with another man."

Romeo's expression darkened. "They understand and they're okay with it."

"Are you?" she asked, lightly touching his arm.

"What? Okay with you parading around the state with your famous ex-boyfriend?"

"With everything. With me interning for the *Westdale Gazette*." Her deal with Crispin gave her an official reason for sticking her nose in other people's murders. A way to appease Romeo while staying true to herself. Her mother had plenty to say about it, of course. None of it good.

He shrugged. "It's who you are. I never thought you were incompetent or helpless, Kit. You know that."

She nodded, her blue eyes sparkling. "And I promise I won't do anything reckless. Not on purpose, anyway."

"Good. We make a great team," he told her. "I'd like to keep it that way."

"Same here," Kit said, the butterflies in her stomach moving at breakneck speed. Months later and he still had that effect on her. "It was nice of your family to host a fake New Year's Eve dinner for us."

"I don't want to ring in the fake new year with anyone except you." His lips brushed her cheek. "Remember the deal. We need to stay until midnight."

"Then you need to keep me awake."

He nibbled her ear. "I can think of ways to do that."

The door jerked open and Romeo bolted upright.

"Romeo Giovanni Moretti," his grandmother's voice boomed. "What kind of gentlemanly behavior is that? Are you trying to disgrace the family in our very own neighborhood?" She grabbed him by the ear and yanked him inside.

"Nonny, you remember Kit."

"Hi," Kit said, following him inside.

Romeo's grandmother looked her up and down with a frown. "I remember. You look better tonight. Your face looks better without all that crap on it."

"Nonny's a little old-fashioned," he whispered to Kit, as though Kit couldn't guess from the older woman's bare, wrinkled skin and plain black dress with knee socks. The orthopedic shoes were the real giveaway, though.

"Mama, you be nice to Romeo's friend." Mrs. Moretti swept into the room and smiled at Kit. "We're so glad you decided to come back. New Year's Eve was too crazy."

"Story of my life," Kit said.

"Come in," Mrs Moretti urged. "I've made lasagna just the way Romeo likes it."

"A little burnt on top," he explained.

Kit noticed Mr. Moretti in the corner of the room in a recliner, reading a book that Kit recognized all too well.

"What do you think?" Kit asked him. "Is he as interesting on paper as he is in person?"

Mr. Moretti set down Charlie's book and peered at Kit over his glasses. "He has certain redeemable qualities."

Kit laughed. "That he does."

"But Romeo's the better man," Mr. Moretti said.

"It's not a competition," Romeo told his father.

"No, it isn't," his father agreed. "Because you already won."

"I sure did." Romeo looked down at Kit, his dark eyes smoldering, and smiled.

***

Thank you for reading The Bitter End! I hope you enjoyed the third book in the Saints & Strangers series. If so, please help other readers find this book ~

1. Write a review and post it on sites like Amazon, GoodReads and LibraryThing.
2. Sign up for my newsletter and check out keeleybates.com so you can find out about the next book as soon as it's available.
3. Like my Facebook page.
4. Don't miss A Sticky End, the next book in the series.

48330622R00101

Made in the USA
Lexington, KY
15 August 2019